THE CLOUD
HUNTERS

D0896772

The CLOUD HUNTERS

ALEX SHEARER

HOT
KEY
BOOKS

First published in Great Britain in 2012 by Hot Key Books
Northburgh House, 10 Northburgh Street, London EC1V 0AT

This paperback edition published in 2013

A CIP catalogue record for this book is available from the British Library.

ISBN: 978-1-4714-0045-2

1

Typeset by Palimpsest Book Production Limited, Falkirk, Stirlingshire
This book is typeset in 11pt Sabon

Printed and bound by Clays Ltd, St Ives Plc

FSC

Hot Key Books supports the Forest Stewardship Council (FSC), the leading
international forest certification organisation, and is committed to printing
only on Greenpeace-approved FSC-certified paper.

www.hotkeybooks.com

Hot Key Books is part of the Bonnier Publishing Group
www.bonnierpublishing.com

For Jane

1

jenine

In the middle of the second term, a new pupil arrived at school. Her name was Jenine and she had two scars on her face, running from under her eyes to just above her mouth. They weren't scars from an accident or scars she had been born with or scars from an attack. They were ornamental. They were the scars of ritual and tradition. And they marked her out as a wanderer, as a nomad: an immigrant of unknown origin; and by tradition such people were Cloud Hunters.

Her family's ship had turned up one day and moored in the harbour. Jenine's father had died – lost in a storm, the rumour said – and her mother commanded the sky-boat now; though in truth there wasn't much to take charge of.

The boat was not large and there was a crew of one, a man so deeply tanned that his skin was almost black. His name was Kaneesh. His ears were studded with rings and he had a single-band tattoo which went all the way around his arm, like a bracelet. His head was shaved and his chest

1

was hairless and he always seemed to glisten, as if he had anointed himself with oil.

Jenine's mother was called Carla, and she, like her daughter and like Kaneesh, had two scars running down towards her mouth. Her hair was jet black and she wore it long and thick, often tied back in a band. She was tall and slim and she looked like a warrior – even when she came to the parents' evenings. She seemed very exotic and the perfume she used smelled strange and unusual. My mother said it was musk. She said it had been taken from the glands of a dead sky-whale, which I thought rather cruel, and bizarre – and somehow intriguing.

Every morning, Carla and Kaneesh would set sail, and every evening they would return. Sometimes the catch had been good; sometimes bad, and they would come back empty-handed, with nothing in the hold.

If they had several bad days in a row, they would journey further afield, which meant that they might not return for a week or more. Carla would then pay somebody to look after Jenine, and to give her board and lodging, so that she would not have to miss school.

She wanted her daughter to have an education. For it's one thing to be a Cloud Hunter because you want to be; it's another thing to be a Cloud Hunter because you have no choice and are qualified for nothing else. Yet, even then, your very looks are against you.

At the weekends, when there was no school, their boat would leave port on Friday afternoon and not return until late on Sunday, or even early on Monday morning, and

Jenine would just be in time for the first lesson. If you asked her what she had done, the answer was always the same.

'We were cloud hunting.'

'You find many?'

'Some. What did you do?'

Well, a whole variety of things. But none of them ever seemed as good, as interesting or as exciting as gliding through mile after mile of clear blue sky, chasing the wisps of distant vapour, speeding towards the faraway patches of cloud, trying to get there before anyone else did, and then coming home with the tanks full of water to sell.

Nothing could compare to that. Not in my eyes. I wanted to go with them, but was afraid to ask, knowing that even if I did ask, I would be refused. Or if I wasn't refused by them, then my parents wouldn't allow me to go.

Yet it wasn't that I lacked the courage to make the journey.

I just lacked the courage to ask to go on it.

It's strange how sometimes it is easier to act than to speak. You'd think it would be the other way round.

Now boys and girls are supposedly different to each other in many more ways than the obvious. And as much as boys may spend a lot of time thinking about girls when they get to a certain age – and vice versa – the fact is that they do not much go around together. At least not until. Until they do, that is. But that was an until which was still a time away.

But in some ways Jenine was like a boy: in the way she thought and the way she acted; so it wasn't so difficult to get to know her. Maybe I even thought that I could capture her, the way her mother's boat captured the clouds, and then I would have the essence of her, possessed and distilled. I thought it would be like chemistry, when you reduce some solution to a mere few droplets and you can hold it in a bottle with a stopper on the top, or in a test tube.

Well, if I did think that, I thought wrong. You can't capture a person that way, or change them from cloud to water. But you can make a friend of them, simply by letting them be and by allowing them to know that you make no claims on them. Then, there you have it – the cloud in your hand, and as long as you don't try to close your fist and your fingers around it, you can keep it; it's yours. But if you do try to hold it, it just slips from your grasp.

I didn't mind the teasing, or if the others said she was my girlfriend, which she wasn't; she was just a friend who happened to be a girl. I didn't overdo it either, or spend too much time talking to her, or make an obvious point of it. I was just friendly, that was all; I was just keeping a friendship warm, just waiting, biding my time, and then one day I would find the courage to ask the question. And with luck, the answer would be yes.

Although now, when I look back, I realise that I had far more than one question to ask.

2

morning

Sometimes I would see the Cloud Hunters leave port, in the cool breath of early morning. It was hard for me to make my steps continue on their way to school after that. They were all I could see, all I could think of. And to me, right there, right then, there could be no finer life, no greater excitement than to be sailing aloft in search of the great, soft, cotton-wool clouds.

But I was just a school student, and my father and mother were administrators and office workers. They wore smart clothes and suits and kept regular hours. They could never have been Cloud Hunters in a million years. For the Cloud Hunters were like gypsies and renegades, with earrings and jewels, hennaed hands and tattoos, bracelets and bands of gold, and with dark, mysterious looks.

They were outcasts and adventurers, and I longed to be one of them, the way that a volunteer, knowing nothing of war, might long to be a soldier. The reality of war, its pain and fear, its terror and discomfort and deprivation meant nothing. All the naive onlooker and would-be recruit could perceive was war's romance.

Yes, I wanted to go with them, wanted to fly away, to chase the clouds, to sail above the sun and into the far reaches of the upper air.

I knew I would never get to go, never, not in a week or a month or a year of Sundays, or any days at all.

But then my chance came, and I took it, and just for a little while I became a Cloud Hunter too.

So that was what happened.

That was my good luck.

And this is my story.

3

traders

My father worked for a merchant shipping company: a sky-trader. There are so many islands here, and their produce so diverse, that there is a constant shuffling of goods between one isle and another.

The trading boats are vast affairs: huge, flat container sky-ships, hundreds of metres long. Or sometimes the cargoes are transported in great barges, one tied to the next, all pulled along in convoy by a tugboat at the front. There are usually a few security outriders too, who patrol up and down along by the barges, making sure that nobody tries to steal anything. There's always the danger of piracy on the high skies. The great container ships and barges ride on the solar wind in a ponderous, stately fashion, making slow but sure progress, lumbering along like pods of sky-whales.

As well as watching out for pirates and hijackers, the patrols have to keep the hulls of the boats free from sky-lice and sky-riders. Sky-riders are small, cat-sized, whiskery creatures, with squashed-looking faces and smooth coats, parasites in their way, that travel by clinging onto the undersides of the boats. They can fly under their own steam when they want to, but mostly they don't. They prefer to travel under your steam instead of their own. They're basically bone idle, and all they want in life is a free ride.

For the most part, they're harmless, or at least they are when it's only four or five of them. But one follows another – as they like to be sociable – and soon, if you're not careful, the whole hull of a boat can be covered in sky-riders, all holding on tight with the suckers on their feet. Soon you've got a colony of them and they're weighing the boat down.

Even one of the great barges can start to sink in the sky, if too many freeloaders latch onto it. Then, as it falls, it will pull the other barges with it, until they all lose buoyancy and suddenly plummet towards the fire of the sun beneath. Then it's too late. Even if the sky-riders abandon the hull to save themselves, the boats go on plunging down under their gathered momentum. Whole cargoes and many lives have been lost that way.

So the outriders constantly patrol the barges on small craft. They keep the sky-riders moving with prods and kicks (for they're thick-skinned and it doesn't do to be too gentle with them) and they try not to let them settle. It's an interminable job at first – you swat them, they come back; you swat them again, they come back again. But once you are out in the Main Drift and far from land, the sky-riders are fewer and you're safe until you approach the islands again.

The strange thing is that, on land, sky-riders are often treated as favoured pets. You find them in people's kitchens, snuggled up in a basket and chewing on titbits, or sitting on their owner's knee. My own grandmother had one. She used to call it Sky-Puss and let it sleep by the window, next to her knitting. But it wasn't much use for anything. If it ever saw a sky-rat, it just stared at it and watched it fly by. It never bothered chasing it. It was simply too much trouble.

Our whole world here thrives on trade. One island grows fruit, another makes machinery. And although most islands are more or less self-sufficient, no single place can produce everything it requires. So there is always travel and great caravans of traders crossing the sky, moving like nomads across a vast desert waste.

And then there's water. Water is wealth and water is prosperity; water is influence; water is power; and water is politics. It's like oil used to be in the old world, so the history books say. Some countries had oil and some did not, and those that did could control the price or trade oil for concessions and favours. Wars were fought over oil, and have been fought here over water too. The richest people in the system are not the ones with the most land; they are the ones who own rivers and reservoirs.

Those islands without natural water sources, or without the wherewithal to collect water for themselves, rely on Cloud Hunters to bring it to them, for both drinking and irrigation. Without this source of supply, many would perish.

There is never a shortage of customers, only ever a shortage of clouds.

I asked Jenine to bring me in some cloud water one day. I wanted to taste it. So she did. They had harvested it just that weekend. It was cool and sweet. You could almost taste the distance in it, taste the adventure of finding it, taste the journey, taste the romance. I told her so, but she said I was mad and that all it tasted of was ordinary water – which isn't much of a taste at all. She said the taste wasn't in the water, it was in my head.

But it didn't seem that way to me.

4

trackers

But a Cloud Hunter's life is not always easy. Sometimes there are long, cloudless weeks and prolonged drought. The vapour doesn't seem to rise and the clouds don't form, and the Cloud Hunters can trek for days on end and see nothing but perpetual blue. Great for your holidays, not so good when you're trying to make a living.

Yet, eventually, if you travel far and long enough, there is always, finally, the haze of herringbone in the distance, or the dense puffballs of dandelion white, just waiting to be harvested and turned into water.

There are times, too, so Jenine told me, when the cloud in the sky is so dense it is like fog. You cannot see where you are going and must navigate on instruments alone. The tanks are soon full of condensed vapour then; your clothes grow damp; your shirt sticks to your back. You fill the auxiliary tanks and wish you had storage for more. Instead of hiding the location of your precious treasure from other Cloud Hunters, you trigger the beacon and radio out a signal to let them know that there is plenty here for everyone, which would otherwise go to waste.

Then you sail for home, your ship almost sinking in the sky, like a swollen balloon, a blister near to bursting. It never ceases to amaze me, the way white clouds turn to clear water and how the insubstantial turns to substance.

There are several different varieties and purities of water too: some to wash with, some to cook with, some only to drink. The latter is sometimes treated like rare, fine wine, and kept bottled in the cellar for special occasions. Connoisseurs sip it and roll it around their tongues, talking of 'good textures' and 'outstanding harvests' and 'vintage years'. So water isn't just water, not to some people – even if Jenine thought it was.

Now, in the old days, in the old world, people used to go hunting for whales. (Real sea whales, not like the sky-whales here.) There was always a lookout then, perched up at the top of the ship's mast in the crow's nest, scanning the horizon, with his hand shielding his eyes and a telescope at the ready. When he saw the spume of foam from a surfacing whale, he'd shout: 'There she blows!' And the captain would turn the ship around and they would set off in pursuit.

With Cloud Hunters it's the same. On every boat there's someone, called a tracker, whose job it is to sense where the clouds are forming and to decide in which direction to travel. Even when the sky is blue and cloudless in all directions, for as far as the eye can see, the tracker knows where to go.

It's a bit of science and a bit of an art – with a little dash of intuition thrown in. Some maintain that it's an instinct or a psychic power. But whatever it is, a good tracker has it, and can sense the formation of clouds as much as four or five days' travelling away. And the captain will always go with the tracker, and point the ship in the direction he says – though you can never know for certain that the clouds will be there. You can only believe. And hope. And sometimes doubt.

For it takes some nerve and courage to journey on into the empty blue, your own water supplies getting lower, and with not a wisp of a cloud in sight. But on you go, sailing on the solar wind. Maybe a breeze blows up, too; so you open the wind sails to catch the uplift and speed on into the void. You pass islands, some above you, some beneath. Some are close enough for you to be in their shadow; others are far below, in regions to which you never venture. There are different, hotter lands down there, with different kinds of people in them. If you went on descending, you would eventually come to islands so blisteringly hot that nothing human lives there, just plants and reptiles and the sky-fish of the deep, with skin like cooked leather. Or so people say. Only, if nothing human can live down there, how would anything human know?

Perhaps, as you sail on, a shoal of sky-fish passes. If you throw a line over the side, baited with a juicy insect or two, you can catch a meal; if you throw a net over, you'll catch a feast.

Or maybe a sky-jelly will come into view, drifting on

the air, almost transparent, a great bulbous mass of pulsating veins. Its tendrils trail underneath it, stretching down for hundreds of metres. As long as it's not one of the poisonous varieties, you can haul it in and cook it. Sky-jellies are mostly water. They may not sound too appetising, but you'll devour them when you're hungry and thirsty enough.

No, a cloud-hunting boat is nothing without a tracker. Sometimes they're referred to as 'divines' – because that is what they do: they divine where the water is, or where the clouds are going to be, or are most likely to form. People used to do this once with hazel twigs to search for wells in droughts and deserts. Hold the Y-shaped twig lightly in your hands; when it swivels and points down, dig at that spot – and there's your water.

Sometimes a tracker's only command is to stay put. They sense that this is the place to be. No need to search for clouds now; they will come to you. So you close the solar panels, reel in the wind sails, and set the satellite anchor to keep you in position.

Then you wait. Maybe for long, silent hours, in the warmth of the sun and the faint stir of the breeze. In the distance a pod of sky-fins gambols by, leaping and capering, always playful, without a discernible care.

Long hours pass and the following hours seem longer still. Waiting takes its toll. You look at the tracker and start to doubt him. His face is inscrutable, his half-closed eyes are small slits in his sunburnt face; or he wears sun-shades and his eyes cannot be seen at all. You sleep, you wake, you take turns at watch, and still the clouds don't come. Then a whole day passes, then two days, three days, four. And still the clouds don't come. Your throat is a dry cavern now, parched as a sand dune. Your voice is a croak. You sound like a frog, but your skin is dry, burning. You roll down your sleeves to cover your arms; you pull down the peak of your hat. You crawl under the canopy and hide in the shade away from the relentless sun.

Another day and your tongue is swollen in your mouth. You can barely swallow, hardly speak. But what's there to say, anyway? And still the clouds don't come.

You look at the tracker, despairing now, accusing. 'You told us to stay here. Had we kept sailing we'd be safe now and the holds would be brimming with water. But no. We're still waiting, and the barrels are dry. And still the clouds don't come.'

The tracker says nothing. He lies in the shade, immobile, inscrutable. Does he really know what he's doing? Or is he also starting to doubt?

Time tries to pass, but it can hardly move; it crawls like a snail on a hot afternoon. A sky-angel swims by, followed by a sky-clown, their markings vivid and surreal, making them seem like the strangest, most miraculous creatures in the universe. Or perhaps you've begun to hallucinate from lack of water.

You move your eyes to watch them, as you lie under the canopy, dry, parched and shrivelled in the everlasting blue. The sky-angels dive to the lower levels. A shoal of ugly-fish takes their place, drab and dreary and boggle-eyed, with faces like bags of stones.

Still the clouds don't come.

And then –

The tracker stirs. He moves a finger; he opens his eyes wider. He smiles and slowly uncoils his legs. You watch him. Why is he moving? There's nothing to move or smile for. But he reaches up and pulls himself to his feet. Yet why does he waste energy in standing? Lie down, man. Don't be a fool.

But then you smell it: cool and moist; you taste it in your mouth; you feel the air grow damp. Drops of condensation wet your lips. Your blackened tongue peeks out, like a starving rat from a hole in the skirting; it tastes water.

Finally you see it. Real? Or a mirage? Your own thirst, maybe, manufacturing illusions?

But no, the cloud is there. It begins to form around you, in wisps and slivers. Soon, it's a thin mist, and then it grows denser and darker. You feel cooler, then cold. Before you know it you can barely see your own hand in front of your eyes.

You shout to the tracker – (oh ye of little faith!) – laughing, drinking in the moisture, wallowing in the damp, clammy cold.

'You were right! It's here now! It's here!'

So now to work. You call to the rest of the crew. The cloud is so thick you can only make out the others as dull shapes on deck. You feel your way to the familiar controls;

you start up the engines and turn on the condensers. The suction pump starts and draws the moisture down into the tanks. It's as if the whole boat were thirsty, gasping for water to save its life. And it gulps and swallows the vapour down with an insatiable, unquenchable appetite.

It takes hours to fill the tanks. You go below to get some waterproofs on or you'll start to shiver. Then back on deck. The hair on your head is as wet as if you'd taken a shower. Visibility is no more than a few metres. The blue of the sky is a memory; the heat of the sun has gone. But the condenser goes on humming, until at last the tanks are full and water is spilling from the overflow and the deck is sopping.

Time to go. You turn the wheel and set a course for home. The tracker sits at the prow, a smile on his face, a well-earned flask of water in his hand and a plate of fried sky-shrimp beside him. He looks at you as if to say, 'You see, I told you so. But you wouldn't believe me, would you? You lost faith. You had your doubts.'

You pretend otherwise, that you never wavered and you believed in him all along, and you always will. But you know that's a lie. There will always be that element of doubt inside you, and, probably, inside him too. Nothing's ever that certain. Even the best of the hunters gets it wrong sometimes. Nobody is infallible; no one always gets it right.

I'm one hundred per cent sure about that.

5

invitation

'I'm inviting someone back for dinner,' I announced one day when I got home from school.

My mother feigned delight. She was always telling me that I ought to be more sociable. But now that it had actually come to it, the inconvenience possibly outweighed the pleasure.

'Oh, that's – that's wonderful,' she said, with just enough hesitation to imply that it might not be. 'Not on a school day, I hope. What with all the homework –'

'Friday,' I said.

You couldn't argue with Friday. There was the whole weekend ahead of it. You couldn't be expected to do homework on a Friday.

'I suppose that will be all right. Who is it? A boy in your year?'

'A girl,' I said.

She looked at me.

'A girl?'

'Yes. But don't panic,' I told her. 'Not a girlfriend. Just a friend, who happens to be a girl. Or a girl, who happens to be a friend. However you want to see it.'

'I see.'

'And I ought to warn you that she's got scars.'

'Scars?'

'Running from here to here.'

'Oh, how awful.'

'No, they're not. They look pretty good.'

'Was it an accident?'

'No. Nothing like that. In fact, they look so good I was thinking I wouldn't mind some myself.'

'Now you listen to me, Christien! Don't you even dare –'

'I was only saying, Mother. I'd never do it,' I admitted. 'It would be too painful anyway. She said they have to drink something first which makes your face go numb, then they get a very sharp knife and they –'

My mother was looking green.

'I think I've heard quite enough. And this is the girl who's coming here? For supper?'

'If that's all right.'

(Well, I assumed she was coming for supper. I hadn't actually asked her yet. She might have been intending to go off with her mother in the boat, but I suspected not. The week had been damp and muggy, with clouds every-where. There was no need for them to go out at the weekend. The boat must have had full tanks.)

'Well, I don't know . . .'

She couldn't say no, though. Had she said no, it would

19

have gone against everything she and my father had always told me – about tolerance and integration and not being prejudiced against minorities and all the rest. So a reserved, 'Yes, I *suppose* so' was the only answer she could give. And that was exactly what I got.

'But I don't know what your father's going to say.'

I couldn't see him saying anything. All I could imagine was him staring at Jenine's mother if she came to the door to collect her daughter after supper, his jaw slowly dropping at the sight of this tall woman with her black hair and green eyes and her scarred face.

He'd probably run a mile.

I thought.

Only it turned out I was wrong.

My mother told him about the invitation later that evening.

'A girl with scars, apparently,' she said.

My father looked up at me from his newspaper, vaguely amused.

'Cloud Hunters?' he said.

I nodded.

'Er – well – yes – I guess so,' I admitted.

He nodded too.

'OK,' he said. 'Ask her round.'

But then I suppose you can't spend your working life around at the Inter-Island Sky Trading Company, supervising the loading and unloading of barges and boats, seeing ships come in from every isle in the system, and not occasionally come across a Cloud Hunter.

Maybe, I thought, I had underestimated him. Maybe my father dealt with people like Kaneesh and Carla on a daily basis, haggling with them over prices and arguing over the quantity of water in a tank or the quality of rice in a hold. The fact that he had not physically travelled so much did not mean that his mind was narrow. He had maybe met more people from more islands than those who had travelled a lifetime. He was fluent in at least five languages, including Common Dialect, and could get by in a handful more.

'Bring her round,' he said. 'Let's see her.'

So I said I would.

But, of course, before I could do that, I had to persuade her to come.

I decided that what it all came down to in the end was being respectable, or at least being seen to be. The appearance of respectability was what my mother cared about. Possibly more than its actuality.

For there was Jenine's mother, with two deep scars on her face and a mass of black ringlets cascading down over her shoulders. And there was her tracker, Kaneesh, who looked as if he would murder you for nothing if you crossed him on a bad day, and murder you for the fun of it on a good one.

And then there was Jenine herself, who not only had facial scars like her mother, but hennaed hands with intricate designs upon them. And though they were doubtlessly three of the kindest and most considerate people, they certainly didn't look it.

21

They looked like – well, what did they look like? You could have said they looked like killers or renegades or refugees from the law. How were my respectable parents ever going to let me go cloud hunting with a crew who looked like that? Had they looked like vicars or singers in a choir, it might all have been easier.

But appearances, of course, can be deceptive. Once you get to know people a little, your prejudices and misgivings about them tend to drop away. You soon discover that you have more similarities than differences. The fact that they smell of musk oil and carry a sharp knife in a sheath on their belt or are covered in scars and tattoos seems eventually not to matter. I was sure my mother would come to see it that way.

Or so I hoped.

It took me a long time to understand something, though – it took half a long voyage that I had yet to undertake. But the fact is that people never see themselves as you see them. They might hate things in themselves that you admire, or value what you perceive as faults. Jenine's scars, for example. In most people's eyes she was strikingly beautiful, and the scars made her even more so. But inside her, things were more complicated. She didn't feel that way about herself and her scars were things she hated. Impossible as it seemed to me, she believed she was ugly.

6

refusal

'No thanks.'

I hadn't anticipated her refusal. I had probably expected her to be delighted, flattered, even.

Here I was, after all, a boy with the hospitality of a fairly big house to offer. We weren't rich, but we were well off. We had a home on the coast with a view of the void, which almost took your breath away every time you looked at it.

If you walked a few steps from our house, you were at the shore. And there, ahead, were views of the other islands, and beneath you was the vast, empty nothingness. It was staggering. It made your head spin and gave you vertigo every time you approached it. But I wasn't afraid of falling, as I could air-swim fairly well; I'd swum at least three or four hundred metres out.

If you think I mean flying by that, well, I don't. It's a different motion, more akin to swimming in water than anything a bird would do. The atmosphere here is thick and heavy, and if you learn the technique properly, you can swim and even float upon the air. If the air of the old earth could buoy up a great eagle, well, here the air can buoy up a person, as long as she knows how to use the currents and the updrafts.

But panic, or lose your nerve, and you'll fall. And the further you fall, the more momentum you acquire, and the harder it is to stop. Until it becomes quite impossible. So you plummet all the way to the fire; though you probably lose consciousness long before you get there – if that's any kind of consolation.

I'd been air-swimming since I was small. There was a wide safety net at the beach near our house, looped from stanchions, which stretched out from the coast. If you lost buoyancy there, it didn't matter. You wouldn't fall far, the net would catch you. Most people learn to air-swim from an early age. Then you're safe and the sky can't harm you; it's just the element around you; it's where you live.

Fathers and mothers take their children to the beaches when they are still only a few months old, to let them have their first taste of swimming in the open air. At that age you're too young to be afraid. But if you leave it until later, when you are old enough to know fear, such a mortal terror can come over you at the sight of that infinite drop that you'll cling to the land and never leave it.

Some islanders have never learned to air-swim and never will. They won't go anywhere near the coast if they can avoid it. And if they ever have to travel, they strap on two or three buoyancy packs, and rope themselves to the deck rails with safety lines. For it's a long way to the bottom, and there's no coming back up. It's even a kind of drowning. You drown in the fire of the sun.

'No?' I was not just disappointed but perplexed. 'Not come for supper? But why not?'

'I might just not want to,' Jenine said.

Well, I supposed that was fair enough, but it still didn't seem like a good enough reason. It didn't even seem like a credible one.

'You can choose what you want to eat,' I said, trying to make the offer more alluring.

'Thanks all the same, but I don't think so.'

Then I understood. Or thought I did. It was her appearance that did it: her clothes, her dark hair and sunburnt skin; the long nails on her fingers, filed and sharpened so that they were almost like talons; and then there were the two facial scars. She looked impregnable, invulnerable. But maybe she wasn't like that inside.

Maybe the most ferocious of appearances actually contain the most sensitive of natures; looks can be deterrents, they are the hard shells around the soft insides.

She was shy, reserved, wary of being out of her element. That had to be it.

And, in the circumstances, why wouldn't she be? We were possibly as strange and as exotic and alien to her as she and her mother and Kaneesh were to us.

She lived on a boat and usually slept on the deck, and

had probably done so most of her life. She had seen her own father tossed overboard in the midst of a gigantic solar storm, so the rumour had it. She had seen him flail and flutter like a leaf in the air, and had watched as he had fallen. Or so I had heard.

Maybe she had also seen the sky-sharks dive and go after him, their fins twitching, their bulbous eyes gleaming, their mouths perpetually ajar, as if they had too many teeth ever to close them properly. Sky-sharks have fins as wide as wings. They never fall, only at the end when they die. They can swim as near to the sun as they can tolerate and they always make it back up.

Despite their fearsomeness, sky-sharks are long and graceful, both menacing and beautiful at the same time. Sometimes they fly so close to land you can see their beady black eyes looking down at you. Should they come too low, people run indoors, or hurry to pick up stones and get their slingshots. But usually it isn't necessary. Sky-sharks don't like people and they don't like land. They're afraid of getting stranded and not being able to take off again.

I'd have liked to have asked Jenine about what had happened to her father. But how do you ask someone a thing like that? You can hardly say, 'Excuse me, but is it true that your father was swept overboard in a storm and got eaten alive by sky-sharks?'

It wouldn't be what you'd call tactful.

So I just tried to persuade her.

'Why not? Why not come?'

'I don't like houses, Christien,' she said. 'Sorry. But they make me feel cooped up and hemmed in. Even the class-room's claustrophobic.'

'But our house is spacious. It's bigger than your boat.'

'Does it have a deck, then?'

'It's got a balcony. We can eat outside, if you like.'

'I do know how to use a knife and fork!'

'I didn't mean –'

'And I don't like people staring at me.'

'No one's going to stare at you.'

'You stare at me. All the time.'

'Yes, but that's different. That's –'

'What?'

Well, I could hardly tell her it was because I couldn't take my eyes off her. So I just denied it.

'My parents are far too polite to stare at anyone,' I said.

'They'll still think things.'

'Yes, like how nice it is to meet you.'

She rolled her eyes. I knew it was cheesy. But say nice things to people and they'll always work – sometimes the cheesier the better.

'We can sky-swim too,' I said, to tempt her. 'There's a beach near my house. With a net. It's quite safe. There's a water pool too. It's not always usable. We can't always afford the water. But there's water in it now. It's not full, but it's deep enough. I mean, it's not a big pool but –'

The thought of the water pool did it.

'OK,' she said. 'I'll come. I haven't swum in water since – oh – for so long I can hardly remember.'

'Do you have a costume?' I said.

'I'm hardly going to swim without one, am I?' she said.

But I didn't know. You never know about Cloud Hunters. They aren't really like the rest of us. They're a different breed. The rules don't seem to apply to them somehow. Cloud Hunters can do what they like.

7

sky-seal islands

Maybe you're wondering how we all travel here, and how we get about between the islands. Well, almost everyone travels by sky-boat, and, in truth, nobody travels fast. It's a leisurely kind of pace. Sky-boats of one sort or another are really the only way to get around. Maybe it's only a trip to the next island, maybe it's a journey of five, ten or fifteen thousand kilometres. But that's how we go.

There are sky-buses and sky-ferries to take you to all the isles in your local sector, and to other sectors too. But long-haul boats don't come by so frequently, and they also cost a lot. So it's best, if possible, to have transport of your own.

Nobody has ever got to the end of all the sectors, or has even mapped them all. The sky just goes on and on. There's no apparent end to it. You could travel all your life, I guess, and still find something new.

Although we live in the sky, aeroplanes would be no good here. Jet engines would soon overheat and burn up in the heavy air. It would be like having syrup in them.

Planes couldn't go faster than the boats anyway, so what would be the point? The boats we travel in float on the air, carried by the wind and powered by the sun.

There are no real continental land masses here, not like in the old world, and there are no oceans or seas at all, not one drop. There are just the islands, circling like satellites at different levels around a fiery core, floating like huge rafts on the heavy air – or bobbing like great flat-bottomed boats in an ocean of sky.

The islands are mostly stable, but sometimes we lurch on the air currents or are battered by rogue thermals and magnetic storms. Then the islands shudder, as if hit by earthquakes. You can feel the ground tremble under your feet and hear the plates rattle in the kitchen cupboards. The motion can make you feel quite sick. But then the island settles again and the nausea soon subsides.

The islands come in all sizes, large and small. Some are only a few hundred metres wide, while others would take days, or even weeks, to cross. Yet they're still only islands. That's all they are: islands in the sky. Even the tiniest of them will remain in place as long as its shape allows it buoyancy. But if it cracks or crumbles, or slips out of orbit and collides with an adjacent island, it can fall, and then it's finished.

Our dense atmosphere is rich in oxygen, but if you were a stranger our air would leave you gasping. Your lungs would struggle just to draw in breath. You'd pant and wheeze, and although the effort wouldn't kill you (unless you had a weak heart) all you would be able to do would be to sit there, trying to inhale and exhale. You'd have the strength for nothing else. You'd be fighting all day, just for breath, until finally you got acclimatised – which might take a month, or even longer.

People have breathed this air for generations, ever since the first settlers came. But it must have been hard for those early pioneers, when they first tentatively lifted the visors from their helmets and looked around them at this brave, new land. But us, their descendants and successors, we've adapted and evolved. We've got lungs like mountaineers.

The temperate islands we inhabit are at the middle level. But there are others both above and below – the lower islands being hotter, the higher ones colder. It is said to snow up on some of the ones above, though I've never been to see it for myself. The temperate zone is a narrow band, in relation to the island world as a whole; just a thin strip of isles, suitable for habitation. The islands far below us are too hot, those high above too chilly. Their climates may have suited other life forms, but not us. We could ascend and descend within certain limits, but anything beyond that and we'd soon die.

Different islands make for different people, and from different temperatures, different temperaments. Why it should be, nobody knows. But that's how it seems to be. Some are bone idle, some are always busy, some are constantly at war, some wouldn't swat an insect.

There is a theory that once, long ago, all the islands were part of the one globe, but then the core erupted and the planet was shattered and blown up out into the atmosphere.

Everything immediately changed, including the density of the air. The core remained but the fragmented pieces never fell back. They went into orbit and here we are.

And then the colonisers came, from other, overcrowded, choked and polluted worlds. They settled the islands, one by one. There was room enough for everyone back then, and there still is. Even now many islands remain unoccupied – perhaps thousands of them.

It might seem an odd way to live, upon a small island in the sky, but to me nothing could be more natural, for it's all I've ever known.

Some of the smaller isles are little bigger than gardens, and a few eccentric people choose to live by themselves on these tiny places, happy – or unhappy – to be on their own. Hermits and recluses set up there, and spend their lives in solitude.

You can see these solitary individuals as you sail by, waving at you in a friendly way, or staring at you threateningly, with a slingshot or a crossbow in their hands, warning you not to get too near and not, for one second, to think of docking.

But they are not always the sole occupants of these isolated clumps of rock. Sky-seals like to bask on them, too: big, fat, blubbery, balloon-shaped creatures, slow moving, with folds of baggy skin, tufts of whiskers and loud, ferocious roars. But they're mostly threats and bluster. They're too fat and lazy to do much, except slip from their rocks when a shoal of sky-fish passes, so that they can grab some easy pickings.

8

swimmers

So Jenine did come to supper, and it was all very polite and civilised (not to say formal and strained, at least in the presence of my parents.) She even left her knife at home on the boat. She wasn't allowed to carry it to school, anyway. But I had seen her at the dockside, and the knife was back on her belt then. Her mother and their tracker, Kaneesh, carried them too.

'She seemed like a nice girl.'

At least that was what my father said, after she had gone. My mother just seemed relieved that she hadn't brought her knife along.

'And I don't know about those scars,' she said. 'Defacing a young girl like that.'

'It's tradition.' My father shrugged. 'You had your ears pierced,' he pointed out.

'That,' my mother said, 'is different.'

I didn't really see why. Less visible, maybe. Not so drastic, perhaps. But it was pretty much the same thing.

*   *   *

Jenine didn't say a lot, not while my parents were there. Nor did she seem all that impressed by anything. But when I showed her my room, her eyes opened wide at the sight of all the stuff. Yet I still had the feeling that she wouldn't have wanted to live there, and that she wouldn't have swapped her bedroll on the deck, or her hammock under the canopy, for all my furniture and gadgets.

After we had eaten, we sat outside a while, then walked down to the cliff edge to see the view. She stood on the very tip of the land, quite unafraid of falling. Beneath her was the safety net, but she didn't seem to like the look of it, as if it might cramp her style. So we walked around the coast until we came to a warning sign, which read: DANGER: EXPERIENCED SKY-SWIMMERS ONLY. There was no net to catch you here, just the emptiness of space beneath you.

She perched on a rock and peered down.

'Come on, Christien,' she said. 'Join me. What are you waiting for?'

I was waiting for the giddiness in my head to go away.

'Well? Are you scared?'

I couldn't let her think that, so I joined her at the edge. I peered down into the vastness.

Beneath us, countless kilometres away, was our sun. Between us and it were hundreds of thousands of islands, all orbiting at different levels. Some were so far away they were little more than spots to the eye. And when you tilted your head back and looked upwards, there were thousands more islands, up above.

Jenine was standing on the very edge of the rock: her heels on land, her toes in space. I grew afraid that she would fall and not be able to save herself. She would panic and forget how to swim. And she would fall and fall, down into the sun, and burn up like a match, leaving a thin trail of smoke and fragments of ash. To fall is instant cremation. Or maybe I would dive after and heroically save her.

'I wouldn't do –' I began.

'You wouldn't do what?'

'Well – I mean – I'd be careful.'

She smiled at me, pretended to totter.

'You worried?'

'No.'

'Yes, you are. What are you worried about?'

'Nothing. I'm not worried about anything.'

'Did you say you had a water pool?'

'That's right. I did.'

We left the shore and walked to the house. I wound back the canopy which covers the pool in order to stop evaporation. It was just under half full. My father had said he would top it up when the price of water fell, or when some rain came. But it was still deep enough to swim in, if not to dive into. We got changed and splashed around for a while and swam a few lengths. Then we lay on the inflatable beds and floated on the water, feeling the warm air on our backs.

'Jenine,' I said.

'Umm?'

'What will you do when the term ends and the long holiday comes?'

'We'll go hunting.'

Of course I knew that. But I wasn't asking for information. I was asking in order to lead up to something.

'How far will you go? Just out for the day?'

'No. Further. Much further.'

'Where will you go?'

She moved her head around on the pillow of the inflatable so that she could see me.

'Why,' she asked, 'do you want to know? Why are you friendly to me, Christien? What are you after?'

I shrugged – which isn't so easy to do when you're lying on a plastic bed in a swimming pool.

'Nothing. I'm not after anything. I just like you. I just ask things because I'm curious. No harm in that, is there?'

'No, I suppose not. No harm at all.'

She drifted up to what would have been the deep end if the pool had been full, then she paddled back with little flicks of her fingers and toes.

'So where will you go?' I persisted. 'Where will the long trip take you?'

'We sail past the Forbidden Isles usually,' she said. 'And on to the Isles of Dissent.'

'Why?' I said.

'We take them water, of course,' she said. 'It's what we always do. Once or twice every turning. With the water we bring them, and what they make for themselves, they can last till we come again. They rely on us,' she said. 'Not many other people will go there. Just Cloud Hunters.'

'Why not? Why won't anyone else travel there?'

'They're afraid.'

'Of what?'

'Of their neighbours. The Forbidden Islanders nearby.'

'But you're not afraid?'

'Of course we are. But we're careful.'

'But you still go, and take water to the Dissenters?'

'If we didn't . . .' Then she trailed off, turned away from me and seemed to doze in the sun.

I flicked water at her.

'Hey!'

She splashed me back, soaking me completely. Girls are like that. Their retaliation is always over the top. They don't just get you back, they get you back tenfold.

'Hey!' I said. 'What did you do that for?'

'You did it to me.'

'That was only a drop.'

'Well, that was a big drop. It'll teach you not to do it again.'

'I wanted you to finish,' I said.

'Finish what?'

'What you were saying.'

'What was I saying?'

'About the Isles of Dissent – you said no one else would go there, and if you didn't take them water. But you didn't say what would happen to the islanders without your water.'

She looked at me through half-shut eyes, scrunched up against the light.

'They'd die, of course,' she said. 'Of thirst. Little by little.'

I left her in peace for a while, then I paddled around to get next to her.

'Jenine,' I said. 'What's it like to go cloud hunting?'

She raised her head and put her hands under her chin.

'I don't know,' she said. 'What's anything like? What's it like to live in a big house by the coast and have your own water pool?'

'I don't know,' I said. 'It's like what it's like, I suppose. It's what you're used to, what you know. But that's not what's interesting, is it? It's what you don't know, that's the interesting part.'

'Umm,' she said. 'Maybe.' Then she rolled off the bed and swam to the steps.

I'd still been hoping that she might invite me to go along with them one weekend. But she didn't take the hint. Perhaps I hadn't been obvious enough. Maybe I needed to do a little underlining.

Jenine's mother came to collect her later. I don't know why she felt it necessary. Jenine was quite capable of making her own way home, and I'd have gone with her anyway. Perhaps her mother was just curious. My father answered the door. He greeted her warmly and invited her in. But she refused politely and said that she ought to be taking Jenine back, as they had an early morning start ahead of them.

My mother came to say hello. Standing next to Carla, she looked like a house-cat next to a tiger. (Not that we have any here, but I've seen pictures.) One was domesticated and one was wild, and each seemed wary of the other; yet they were of the same species, if but distantly related. But they were polite enough. My mother is fond of saying that all you need to be is polite. She thinks it will get you out of anything.

Jenine said goodbye and she and Carla walked off together. They didn't look back, not once. I watched until they were out of sight. They looked like two tigers, mother and cub, loping along, both lithe and slender, moving with feline grace.

As they walked away, two sky-fins came into view, about five or six hundred metres above, gambolling and frolicking. They swam off to the left and a few minutes later a sky-shark appeared. It seemed to be tracking them, and it headed in the same direction. If it found them, then the following morning the land beneath would be flecked with blood.

Next week at school, Jenine didn't say a word about the visit. And as for taking hints, I realised that I could give her a hundred and she would never take any one of them. If there was something that I wanted, I would simply have to ask for it outright.

'If you don't ask, you don't get,' my father used to say. 'And even when you do ask, you don't always get. But at least you're in with a chance, aren't you?'

I disagreed with him on a lot of things, but I agreed with him on that.

9

the forbidden isles

The Forbidden Isles – I'd better briefly tell you about them. They're a string of islands to the east of the Main Drift, just beyond the Islands of Night. (The Main Drift is our major highway; it's a sky-road that can take you almost anywhere.)

The next thing I'll say about the Forbidden Isles is that they didn't get their name for nothing. And the third thing I'll tell you is that if you don't have to go there, you don't want to.

And if you do want to, you must be mad – as mad as the Forbidden Islanders. And that's saying something. Because they've got every variety of patented insanity there; there's one kind for every island and an island for every one.

The islands aren't 'forbidden' in the sense that you may not go there. You can go whenever you please, just as long as you strictly observe the local customs. But, if you don't, it's at your own peril, and you may never get to leave.

It's true that a handful of the Forbidden Isles admit no visitors at all. And it is obvious which ones they are. Their coastlines are bordered with floating sky-mines. Bash into one of those and your ship will be smithereens. Bits of you will be turning up a thousand kilometres away.

But generally speaking, the Forbidden Isles are called 'forbidden' because of what is prohibited there. Or, conversely, because of what is strictly insisted upon. Or sometimes both.

In the Northern Forbidden, for example, women must never cut their hair; it must always be long enough to cover their ears. In the Southern Forbidden all men must be clean shaven and never sport beards. The punishment for Northern women trimming their hair is to have their ears chopped off. The punishment for Southern men growing beards is to have their noses sliced. Most people (especially short-haired women and bearded men) try to avoid these islands. And so it goes on similarly elsewhere. There are islands where men must always cover their heads and where women must not – sitting right next door to islands where women are forbidden to wear hats of any kind, and men must go bare-headed.

The Forbidden Isles are not famous for tolerance either. They're home to all the bigotry and weirdness you can think of. Yet anybody can land on them, who is prepared to take their chances or who is willing (at least temporarily) to conform.

The main chance you take is that you might not get away again. For you could all too easily be swept up in one of their quarrels, or be arrested for a spy, to spend the next twenty years in a cell the size of a large dustbin.

41

And they'll think they're treating you kindly if they give you bread and water every other day, and allow you use of the prison toothbrush once a month; the toothpaste ran out long ago. The punishments for contravening local customs can be severe, including being tied to posts on the tops of hills and being left there for the sky-sharks.

The inhabitants of any one Forbidden Isle never seem to agree, almost as a matter of principle, with the views, practices or opinions of their neighbours. In fact, they go to war with each other on a regular basis. (None of them seems to forbid that.)

They are the most aggressive and intolerant people in the whole system. No other sector is like it, or as dangerous. In a world where there is space and an island for everyone, the Forbidden Islanders cannot seem to stomach the idea that anybody else could be entitled to be different.

In fairness, visitors are usually given plenty of warning of knowing what they are letting themselves in for. There are notices up in every port and harbour, defining local customs. You can't miss them. They're there telling you that women should remove all headgear or that men must put some on, or whatever it might be. And these are more than quaint local customs; these are matters of life and death.

In the Lower Eastern Forbidden, for example, all people must wear gloves. Nobody really says why, except that it is allegedly unclean not to do so. The punishment for not covering a hand is to have the uncovered one chopped off. You may only remove your gloves when at home in the presence of your family. To remove your gloves in the presence of anybody else is considered deeply offensive and punished accordingly. There are people on the island with no hands at all. And nobody has any sympathy for them, for they brought it all on themselves.

But the ludicrous wars and quarrels of the Forbidden Islanders have a serious side: they make travel through the area, and trade within it, extremely dangerous. The Forbidden Islanders take the view that if you are not for them, then you are against them – you are for their enemy, which makes you their enemy too.

So it's as well to give the Forbidden Isles a wide berth. For you never know what odd cult is going to spring up next. You may find that someone has taken a dislike to other people breathing, or talking, or whistling, or eating lunch. And if they find you doing any of these things, they'll kill you. Just to show you the error of your ways.

Now, next door to the Forbidden Isles are the Isles of Dissent. And the contrast could not be greater.

These neighbouring islands are where those who couldn't agree with bigotry or live with tyranny took refuge and set up their own societies. Whatever their individual views may be, their main precept is tolerance. They don't wish to kill anyone for thinking differently. They just want to live in harmony.

Their essential philosophy seems to be that the majority is always wrong, and that absolute certainty is usually a mistake, and that people should always budge up and make a little room for doubt. (Although they cannot, of course, be absolutely sure of that, for it would invalidate all they believed in.)

The Dissenting Islanders are the most easy-going people in the system, and their Forbidden Isle neighbours regard them with deep suspicion and hostility. They also refuse to trade with them or to supply them with water.

The Isles of Dissent, though beautiful, are barren and dry. Little flourishes there naturally except some bitter, inedible weeds. The Dissenters grow what food they can in greenhouses, but these require irrigation. They make some water using condensing machines to extract it from the air; but the local atmosphere is so lacking in humidity that they collect very little.

Once or twice a month it might rain. The Dissenters collect and store all they can. They use their water frugally, and reuse it, over and over. They filter and distil used water to make it clean again; not a drop is wasted.

If so much as a cup of water is knocked over, it is a cause of much dismay and recrimination. Small children are kept well away from water containers; it's not the stuff to play with.

You might imagine that with such a shortage of water, the Dissenters would have a strong, pungent aroma about them. But they are as clean as anyone. It is just that where some people would use a bath, they make do with a bowl; where others would use a shower, they use a flannel.

But their biggest fear is not the bigotry of the neighbouring Forbidden Islanders, nor that they might suffer from body odours and stale sweat. Their major fear is fire, for they do not have the water with which to extinguish it.

The Dissenters rely on visits from Cloud Hunters to keep themselves and their horticulture alive. No other traders will risk passing the neighbouring Forbidden Isles. The Cloud Hunters are the only ones.

So I wondered long about what Jenine had said to me, about taking water to the Isles of Dissent when the main school holiday came. It sounded like an adventure and a half. And I wondered how they intended to go there.

The simplest, safest route was along the Main Drift. But this way was also indirect and tedious and time-consuming. The quickest course was between the Islands of Night. But few went that way if they could avoid it. Especially since the people who did go that way stopped coming back.

That route also took you close to the Forbidden Isles, who were at war with each other again, and suspicious of all strangers – whose presence might unite even them in common cause. One look at Kaneesh and the Forbidden Islanders would have the grappling irons on the deck, the boat boarded in minutes.

The trouble with Kaneesh was that he looked too much like the heathen he was, all the way from his head to his toes. I'm not saying he was a heathen in any bad sense. He just seemed like a general affront to organised society, and an intolerant one certainly wouldn't stand him for long. And although he looked well able to take care of himself, there was only one of him. Even he couldn't have taken on a warship full of Forbidden Islanders single-handed.

Cloud Hunters, as a breed, are an independent and a fearless race. They travel where they please and trade with whom they choose. Cloud Hunters are afraid of nobody. Or rather, they more than likely are, but they know how to conceal it. And sometimes the appearance of fearlessness is as good as fearlessness itself.

I think the Cloud Hunters shared the Dissenters' view that the majority was always wrong, that the law was always in need of reform, that all certainties needed rethinking and that everything forbidden should perhaps be allowed after all.

And they could have sold their water anywhere. They didn't have to trade with the Isles of Dissent. It was a long, hazardous journey, but they made the voyage regularly, without fail. And that water they delivered was just enough for the Dissenters to scrape by on, until they came again.

The Dissenters sometimes tried to hunt clouds for themselves, but never with much success. They had neither the equipment, the traditions, nor the expertise. Also, their neighbours, the Forbidden Islanders, with their compressors and distillers, sucked every cloud up almost the moment it appeared.

Once or twice there had been clashes between them over this, but the superior forces of the Forbidden Islanders had blasted the Dissenters out of the sky.

When it comes to war, you can bank on it that the pacifists never win.

10

men-of-war

If you don't ask, you don't get.

So I decided it was time to do some asking. Maybe for just a little at first, then a bit more. What did I have to lose, apart from the breath it took to ask the question?

A refusal may often offend. But I wasn't that easily offended, at least not by a simple No. It could change to a Yes at any time. All it needs is a little persistence. That's the way to change people's minds: keep at them. Just look at a little child who wants an ice cream, when his parents say no. He rants, he raves, he lies on the ground, he holds his breath until his face turns blue. And maybe it gets him nowhere. Or sometimes it gets him his ice-cream cone.

Besides, nobody else had invited Jenine to visit their homes or to splash in their half-empty water pools. Almost everyone else in the school was wary of her, and those who weren't were often snobs, who wouldn't have allowed a Cloud Hunter anywhere near the house anyway, unless it was to deliver water. And even then they'd have told them not to come in, but to wait outside on the inaptly named welcome mat.

I thought I'd start by being subtle.

I ran into Jenine one morning, and asked when she might next be embarking on a cloud-hunting expedition.

'The weekend, I would think,' she said. 'Depends on the weather.'

'Well, that would be a nice trip,' I said. 'I've never been cloud hunting myself.'

'Haven't you?' she said. 'No, I don't suppose you have. Not being a Cloud Hunter, and not having a cloud-hunting boat, it's not that likely, is it?'

And that was that. So much for subtle hints.

The following morning, I tried again. My father had happened to drop a useful piece of information while we had sat talking at the dinner table the night before.

'Hi, Jenine.'

'Hi.'

'Jenine –'

'What?'

'Is it true that according to Cloud Hunters' custom, hospitality must always be reciprocated?'

'What?'

'You know – that one invitation deserves another.'

She looked as if she might break into a smile, but didn't.

'Been doing research, have you?' she said. 'Into the quaint customs of minorities?'

'No, just – happened to hear about it.'

'What are you getting at, Christien?'

'Well, as I invited you to dinner – you know –'

'You want your invitation returned? You want to eat what we eat? Rice and sky-fish from a bowl? With a pair of chopsticks? Sitting cross-legged on the deck? Wouldn't you miss your nice cutlery and comfy chairs? And we're a bit short on napkins.'

'Wouldn't mind. But I'd rather come for longer than dinner.'

'Oh, would you? Meaning what, exactly?'

'How about I come cloud hunting? One weekend?'

'You?'

'Yes.'

'What would you do?'

'Get in the way.'

'Yes, you probably would.'

'No, I'd be useful. I could help out.'

'Help? Doing what?'

'If you showed me what to do I could be useful.'

'Hmm –'

'Is that a yes, then?'

It wasn't.

'I think I go this way, here,' she said. 'And you go that way, don't you? I'll see you around.'

But she hadn't actually said no. When I tried the third time, she just shrugged and said she'd ask her mother, if she remembered, that was.

Just in case she hadn't remembered, I reminded her again the next day.

*　　*　　*

It was another week before I received a proper answer. But it had been worth waiting for.

Jenine came up to me one lunch hour and said, without preamble, 'We're sailing this weekend, if you want to come, in the late afternoon. We'll be away two nights. You'll need to bring a bedroll. Be there no later than five. We shan't wait. If you're not there, we'll just go. We'll be back about six in the evening, Rest Day night.'

And that was it.

Rest Day was another expression for the old Sunday. The names of Sunday through to Saturday fell into disuse. We divide our time up just like people used to; and we kept the number of days but changed the names. Rest Day is the old Sunday, First Day is the old Monday, and you can no doubt work out the rest for yourself.

I went home, worried about getting permission to go off at such short notice. My father would look concerned and my mother would no doubt say, 'What about your homework? Is it safe? Cloud Hunters, are they reliable? Are they the sort of people you can trust?'

And so on. But I had some replies ready – antidotes to every objection. I could do my homework on the boat. Of course they were respectable, she had met them, hadn't she? Of course they were trustworthy; a Cloud Hunter's word was a gilt-edged bond. Of course it was safe, they were reputedly the best sailors in the whole system. And Kaneesh looked able to handle any trouble. And so did Carla come to that and – and so on.

So I asked as soon as I got home.

My parents said they'd think about it.

It seems to me that some people are a little overly fond of thinking about things. Maybe a bit less thinking things over and a bit more decision-making wouldn't be a bad idea.

While they were thinking about it, there was an emergency warning on the news. We were used to them; they didn't really worry us. But this time it was different. A merchant sky-trader had spotted two men-of-war in the vicinity of the island, two sky-jellies that is, and from the way the prevailing winds were blowing, they were heading in our direction. They might pass the island by, or they might sail overhead. We just had to be on the alert and ready to take cover the moment their approaching shapes triggered the sirens and sent people scurrying inside.

Nine times out of ten the warnings amounted to nothing: the men-of-war would be blown away from us, or they might rise on a thermal, far above us, or even drop underneath our island as they hit a current of cold air.

People give familiar names to unfamiliar things – perhaps they feel somehow reassured by it – and the sky-jellies were no exception. Like the jellyfish in the sea of the old world, some of these creatures were small and harmless, but others were huge and lethal, and trailed long, poisonous tentacles.

These men-of-war were the largest, their dimensions staggering. They could be as big as whole islands. Their tentacles would drift for astonishing distances. It could take a day for a giant man-of-war to pass overhead. And until it did, there was nothing you could do but to stay inside and wait for it to go. If one of its tentacles touched you, it would scar you for life, possibly kill you, and your death would be a prolonged and an agonising one. Their tentacles held sacs of poison.

Even after a man-of-war had passed, it left trouble behind it. Its drifting tentacles would attach to buildings and rocks, and then tear away as its vast, translucent body floated off with the breeze. The loss of a few tentacles seemed not to bother it in the slightest.

The discarded tentacles would lie, matted on the roofs and dangling from the sides of buildings, trails of slimy jelly, corrosive and dangerous to touch. The fibrous covering held in the moisture, so the remains would take a long time to evaporate. They had to be neutralised with chemicals and then burnt away, or scraped off, by workmen wearing thick gloves, protective suits and goggles.

The gunge would be everywhere, on your doors and windows, on the walls of your house, on the doorbell, the door handle, on the garden path. It was horrible stuff and had a bad odour, smelling every bit as foul as it looked.

We were lucky that the men-of-war jellies didn't pass by often. There were frequent warnings, but mostly came to nothing. The wind would change direction and the men-of-war would drift elsewhere.

Sometimes a gunship would go up and try to create enough air turbulence to make them alter course. Or it would simply blast them out of the sky – fragments of poisoned jelly splattering everywhere. Then down they would go.

The sky-jellies often had babies with them: small pulsating things, no bigger than kites, their tentacles only a few feet long and as pretty as paper streamers. The babies even looked quite cute. Instead of being wholly transparent, they were vivid red, with traces of pink. But they were every bit as poisonous.

I was out by the beach when the siren sounded. I could see the blob in the distance, far off in the sky. There was plenty of time to get home, but I ran.

When I got back, both my parents were there – home from work early. We locked the doors and windows and I went up to my room. I sat there, with my elbows on the sill, peering out, as the sky gradually darkened and a convoy of men-of-war drifted into view. I wondered what Jenine was doing. I guessed she and her mother and Kaneesh would have battened all the hatches and be sheltering in the cabins of their boat.

The men-of-war came, their tendrils leisurely trailing across the rooftops, like fingers stroking a face. The first wave of them passed without incident, but then a second wave came. These were larger, floating lower in the sky. Their tendrils dragged all over the island, leaving globules of slime.

I watched them float towards our house. Then I heard a voice – the voice of a panic-stricken man shouting. He must have somehow ignored the early warnings – or hadn't heard them – and become trapped outside.

He was running, terrified, over the fields, with the men-of-war right behind him. Their tentacles dangled like those bead curtains they have in the doorways of food shops, to allow the cool air in, but to keep the insects out.

He ran, shouting for help, desperately seeking shelter. He beat on doors and hammered on windows, but nobody would dare to let him in.

On he ran, the men-of-war following, moving swiftly with the wind. The man tripped and fell; he got up, stumbled again, then got up once more. He limped on, hobbling painfully, as if he had twisted an ankle.

The men-of-war were gaining on him, yet floating with such effortless grace. They looked so beautiful it was hard to believe they were dangerous. They could have been the great blooms of giant flowers.

The man hurried limpingly on. I lost sight of him for a moment, but then heard his cries again, and I could hear him begging for help as he hammered at our door, the last house around. There was no other shelter.

I dashed to the stairs, but my father was already in the hallway. He yanked the front door open and pulled the man inside. The man tumbled in and collapsed on the floor. My father slammed the door shut, just in time, for a second later there was the soft, flaccid sound of scraping tendrils dragging along outside. The house grew so dark it was almost like night. We turned on the lights; we waited; we listened. At last the sky lightened. The men-of-war had passed. Our windows were smeared with slime.

My father helped the man up and took him to the

kitchen, where my mother bandaged his ankle. She offered him some tea, but my father poured out rum. The man thanked us profusely.

When we saw him out, we discovered that the paintwork on the outside of the door had peeled and blistered where the sky-jelly had brushed against it. It was like the scar of a burn mark, and gave off a bitter, acrid smell.

We stared at the mark, and though nobody said anything, we were all thinking the same thing: that it could so easily have been the man and not the door; that he might now be lying there on the doorstep, in the final throes of death.

At least they had passed, though, and we wouldn't see them again for a long while.

Or so we hoped.

But the wind changed direction. And they came back.

And this time it was Jenine they came for.

11

deadly waltz

We were at school next morning when the men-of-war returned.

First we heard the sirens, telling us to get inside and to close all doors and windows. Then we saw them come. The siren stopped and the world fell to silence. The teachers locked the outer doors.

We gathered at the windows to watch them. It was a free show. They were riding the thermals and rippling with the wind. They blocked half the light. Silence fell, heavy and thick, like a blanket; it seemed to envelop the whole island. We jostled for space to get a decent view. Some people stood on their desks, but the teacher let them and said nothing. We watched, and waited, and listened.

Jenine was in front of me, next to the window. I watched her face as the men-of-war came. She was almost radiant. Most of the others looked awed or apprehensive. But Jenine just smiled, as if she and the sky-jellies were part of something from which the rest of us were excluded: some natural wildness, something raw and dangerous.

'Aren't they beautiful?'

'Beautiful as in deadly,' I told her.

She didn't answer me. Just kept watching.

Maybe it was that they were both travellers and drifters; maybe it was that they were untrammelled and free; maybe it was any one of a thousand things, but she smiled to see them coming, as though they had an affinity, an understanding.

The men-of-war were low in the sky now.

'There must be hundreds of them,' someone said.

'Thousands!'

'Millions!'

I guessed there were about sixty. Some were fully grown adults, others were half developed, others seemed newly born. They floated towards us, tendrils trailing, bodies translucent. You could see their eyes, their veins. Their very hearts were visible through their clear, outer layers; you could see those hearts beating, clenching like fists, then relaxing, then clenching again, pumping blood.

They all moved so languidly on the air. They could have been massive water lilies floating on a pond. On they came, like an invading army of flowers.

There was something condescending about them too. It was more than their mere height above us, it was something else, something about the lazy, graceful way they moved which made you feel clumsy, earth-bound and inept. They looked down on us, vast and superior, indulgent, impassive, cryptically smiling Buddhas.

Yet according to what I had read, they were barely even conscious of their own existences. What brains they had were disproportionately tiny; what intelligence they had was small. When you looked up at one you could see its eyes and heart and digestive tract quite plainly, but as for a brain, it was hard to know where it was.

It was probably that small grey blob of matter behind the eyes, the size of a large sky-shrimp. It was hard to believe that creatures so huge, so beautiful and so dangerous were also intrinsically rather stupid, with not much more intellect than a vegetable and possibly less than an insect.

All the same, it was quite a sight.

'Barely conscious of their own existence,' I said. 'Brains so small they don't even know they've got one.'

Jenine turned and glanced at me.

'I've met a few people like that,' she said.

'Yes,' I agreed. 'Me too.'

The first of them hit.

Its tentacles collided with the window. The glass was reinforced, precisely for such contingencies. But instinctively we ducked. Somebody fell off the desk they had been standing on.

There were shouts and a few tears. We could hear the wails of the younger children coming from one of the other classrooms and then the comforting voice of their teacher, reassuring them that it would all soon pass, that there was nothing to be afraid of, that everything would be all right.

The tentacles brushed the window, held on momentarily, then slithered away, leaving globs of mucous to run down the glass.

'Eeech!'

It really was disgusting. They weren't called jellies for nothing.

The sky was full of them now, like a fiesta of hot-air balloons. It would take a good hour or more for them all to pass. Our teacher let us watch a while longer, then began to say that we ought to get back to some work.

She was telling us to return to our seats when we heard it. It came from outside. It was the sound of something small and whimpering. I looked out and saw a little dog. It belonged to the janitor's children. It was outside their house, across the yard. The dog sat on its haunches, gazing up at the darkened sky, whimpering pitifully as a tendril trailed towards it, full of malignant poison.

We watched, transfixed, as the tendril came. It dragged in the dirt. The dog sat, still whimpering, too petrified to move. There was a small wet puddle under it, spreading out. The animal stared up at the sky, bewildered, mystified, immobile with terror. The tendril passed. It missed the dog by a few centimetres. But more were on the way.

'Somebody should do something!' a voice said.

Only who? Who was going to risk their neck? For the sake of a dog?

A girl was crying.

'The dog, the dog, the poor dog!'

And of course, we all had sympathy for it, but there was nothing we could do. I watched, with grim fascination and – if I am honest – a certain amount of pleasurable and anticipatory dread. It was like the excitement of watching a fictional horror drama unfold, at some moment of high suspense – like watching the man on the high wire, wondering if he would fall off. Only this was real. I didn't want the dog to die. Nobody did. But we all saw that its death was inevitable. The men-of-war were so densely packed overhead now that their bodies were touching. They pressed against and bounced away from each other like fat balloons, clearly immune to each other's poison.

Their tendrils hung like creepers, like vines. It only needed one of them to touch the soft coat of the small dog. Then the puppy would emit a shrill, sudden whelp as the acid poison ate into it, and it would be over and done with.

She jumped down from the desk.

'Jenine,' I said. 'What are you doing?'

'Well, if no one else will do anything –'

And she was gone before anyone could stop her. The door banged behind her. The teacher shouted.

'Hey!'

Too late. The key had been left in the door. The next moment, there Jenine was, outside, running across the school yard. The teacher banged on the window.

'Jenine! Get back in here!'

But Jenine didn't hear, or she didn't want to. She ran towards the dog. It saw her coming, and decided to do the one thing that wouldn't help either of them: it ran away. It ran back, towards the approaching curtain of tendrils, hanging like thousands of ribbons from the men-of-war up in the sky.

'Jenine! I order you now . . . !'

Wasted words. Jenine went after the dog and cornered it. It yapped and whimpered, its little legs strutting almost comically as it tried to get away from her and back out into the very danger she was trying to save it from. She grabbed it by its collar, and scooped it into her arms. Then she turned to run back with it to safety and shelter.

Only it was too late. The men-of-war were above her, their tendrils dangling; she was surrounded.

No one spoke. We watched from behind the safety of the windows.

The dog had fallen silent and ceased to struggle. It seemed to find some comfort in her arms. She stroked its head and talked softly to it. She stood and waited – waited for death.

But then she began to sway, and strangely, it seemed, to dance.

Of course, it wasn't a dance at all, but that was how it looked. She stood where she was, watching the tendrils approach. But then she moved aside as one came, and the moment it had passed, she moved her hips to avoid another. The passage of the tendrils seemed to make her figure shimmer, like a mirage on a heat-hazed horizon. The tentacles even seemed to reach out for her, like supplicating hands, but she eluded their grasp.

I could hardly breathe. We all watched, silent and fascinated, expecting at any instant to hear her scream and the yelp of the dog as the two of them became entangled in that forest of poison, that hanging-garden canopy of death.

But no sound came. The men-of-war passed above her, their tendrils trailing on the ground. They twisted and writhed, and as they did, Jenine twisted and writhed around them. They even seemed to dance with her, passing her on as a partner from one to the other, as each tendril waltzed with her a moment, then made its bow, and the next one took its place.

How long we watched and how long she swayed and danced away, I don't really know. It was probably no more than minutes, but it seemed like hours.

Finally, they had gone. The all-clear sounded. Jenine stood alone in the yard, with the small dog still cradled in her arms. There were globs of poison lying on the ground. She carefully stepped over and around them and walked to the school building. Somebody opened the door and let her in. We heard the dog barking; and then the door to the classroom opened and Jenine entered. Her arms were empty. She must have given the dog to one of the teachers.

Without a word to any of us, she returned to her seat, took some books out, and waited for the lesson to resume. The men-of-war had all moved on and the sky was clear. The janitor was already out in the yard, shovelling neutraliser over the globs of poison.

Our teacher looked as if she felt she had to say something – something pointless and predictable, such as, 'That was a very dangerous and a very foolish thing to do, Jenine. You could have been killed!'

But the words didn't come out. She knew, as we all knew, that what Jenine had done had been more than dangerous and foolish. It had been fearless and courageous too.

The teacher went over to her and touched her on the shoulder.

'Well done, Jenine,' she whispered. 'That was brave. Reckless – but brave.'

Jenine's face remained as impassive as ever. She just smiled very slightly and then opened up her books to be ready to start work. I looked intently at her, at her sunburnt skin and her perfectly proportioned face, at the deep, disfiguring scars which ran from her high cheekbones down towards her mouth. I'd never seen or known anyone like her in my life. I'd have followed her to the ends of the world.

I felt that I should have gone out and tried to save the dog myself. That I had been a coward for not doing so. But I also knew that if I had done, I would now be lying dead on the tarmac of the yard, with acid burns over my body and poison on my skin. And the dog would be as dead as I was. So what would have been the point?

Dancing was not my strong point.

And anyway, heroism is not much without skill. It can be just a pointless sacrifice or an empty gesture. But Jenine had been more than stupidly brave, she had known what to do, and how to do it. She had never intended to throw her life away for a dog. She had intended to save it. And she had.

Maybe, like the men-of-war, she, too, was wild and free. But unlike them, she had a brain.

I got a word with her later, as we were going home.

'That was pretty brave, Jenine,' I said. 'If a bit stupid.'

'Pretty much the same as you then,' she said. 'Only maybe the other way round.'

It took me a moment to figure that one out. But she was smiling. So I assumed it was meant as a joke.

'So are you coming with us?' she asked. 'We'll be sailing this weekend. Are your parents all right about it?'

'Er – they've not actually said yes yet. But I'm hoping they will – imminently,' I said.

'You live in hope a lot, don't you, Christien?' she said.

'Yes,' I had to concede. 'I guess I do.'

Only she didn't know even the half of my hopes. Nor how much she was a part of them.

12

people like that

My father was impressed when he heard the story, but my mother less so.

'Sheer madness,' she said. 'Risking your life for a dog.'

'But they're plainly courageous people, these Cloud Hunters,' my father said to her. 'And resourceful. He's bound to be safe with people like that, to go away with for a few days.'

'People like that, indeed,' my mother repeated, but with altered emphasis. You could hear the italics in her voice.

She really didn't approve of *people like that*. *People like that* had too many tattoos, scars and earrings; they used knives more than forks and didn't always say 'excuse me' when they left the table (when they had a table to leave).

'I can't see the harm in his going,' my father said. 'It's only for the weekend, after all.'

'What about his homework?'

'He can do it before he goes.'

'Not if they're leaving immediately.'

'Then he can do it on board. He'll have hours to fill while they're travelling. After all, there aren't any clouds here, are there? It'll probably be a ten-hour journey before they catch sight of one. And besides, when and where does the girl do her homework? On the boat, I presume.'

'If she does any homework,' my mother retorted. (Because they wouldn't bother to do any homework, would they? I thought. Not people like that.)

'She does do her homework,' I said. 'As a matter of fact she always does it.'

I could have added that she usually came in among the top five in class. But then I would have been asked why I didn't, and that wasn't a debate I wanted to get into right then.

'Come on. Let's say he can go,' my father said indulgently.

'Well . . .'

That was a good sign. My mother was running out of objections and her objections were running out of steam.

'Oh, all right. Just this once then – I suppose. But you'd better make sure you do your homework, that's all.'

That was my mother. She wasn't so bad. She just hated to make a concession. And if she ever did make one, she always liked to qualify it. You could go, but you had to do your homework. You could eat some sweets, but then you had to brush your teeth. Or you had to have fruit first. There was always some condition.

There were days when I felt it was a pity that my parents hadn't had more children. Then she would have had someone

66

else to focus on apart from me. Nagging shared would be nagging halved, I reckoned. But I was their only child.

Most families only had one child: little emperors and empresses, that was us. It was the water: everyone was afraid of drought. So many mouths to feed and only limited water to go round. There had been a long drought once, some fifty years back. Half of the memorial stones in the Field of Remembrance dated from that time.

It was hard to imagine what it had been like to live in the old world, on a planet that was mostly water. Yet even there, so the history books said, there had been deserts, in a place that was nearly all river and sea. I felt that somebody wasn't telling the truth. It was only later I discovered that the seawater was tainted with salt and undrinkable, and the rivers were polluted. There had been pure ice caps once too, but they had all melted.

'So I get to go?' I said to my mother,

'I suppose so. But –'

I don't remember what the but was. I never listen to the buts if I can avoid it. If you start listening to all the buts you'll never go anywhere or do anything. You'll find your-self butted into an armchair and you'll never dare to get up from it for fear of all the things that might happen to you if you did.

And then what have you done with your life, apart from been good and done what was expected of you and always kept your nose clean? All very fine and admirable things in their way. But they aren't everything, are they?

I had permission to go and I was going. Just as long as Jenine hadn't changed her mind in the meantime, or her mother hadn't changed it for her. As for Kaneesh, their tracker, I'd probably be a useless encumbrance, as far as he was concerned. He didn't seem to think much of anyone who wasn't a Cloud Hunter. But then you can't please everyone, no matter who you are, and it's a mistake even to try.

Sometimes Kaneesh would stand on the boat deck, down at the harbour, throwing his knife at the mast, trying to hit a small circle he had carved there. He never missed.

When he tired of throwing the knife with his eyes open, Kaneesh would close them. Still he never missed. Or he would turn his back to the mast and throw the knife over his shoulder. I saw him miss once that way. But only once. He didn't miss the next time.

Those were Kaneesh's only amusements and occupations as far as I could tell: watching for clouds, rolling dice, throwing his knife at the mast. I never saw him read anything, or was even sure that he could read much – apart from the history and the narrative of the sky, the approach of clouds and the formation of vapour.

I think the sky was like a book to him: a vast kaleidoscopic volume of innumerable pages, that told some unending, and constantly changing, story. It never bored him and he never seemed to tire of reading it. It was fiction and fact, poetry and reference, religion and entertainment, mystery and encyclopedia, all rolled into one.

You'd often see him at the harbourside, itching to set

sail, sitting on the tethered boat, staring out into the distance as if he'd spied a cloud fifty kilometres away and couldn't wait to get to it.

He seldom turned his eyes towards the land or looked with any curiosity at the people upon it. Land and people were a waste of time. All that mattered to him were clouds, as if they had more substance than anything.

At other times he would just sit on deck, throwing dice, over and over, as if the numbers were going to tell him something. But what they told him, he kept to himself.

I wondered sometimes about Kaneesh and Jenine's mother, Carla. I wondered if he had taken her father's place. But he didn't seem overly familiar, so it was hard to tell. Carla was plainly still the boss, as owner of the boat. Sometimes she was tetchy and abrupt with him as she issued orders – commands which he either studiously ignored or only condescended to follow in his own good time.

Occasionally they quarrelled. You would see them on the boat, Kaneesh with his arms folded, stubborn and immovable, while Carla ripped into him with a torrent of reproach or abuse or who knew what it was? When she was angry she didn't speak any language I could understand, but reverted to some dialect that must have come with her ancestors when they arrived with the first colonisers, all those years ago. They were nomads, even back then.

I wasn't sure if even Kaneesh could understand her. But it didn't really matter. Her gestures, tone and body language told you all that you needed to know: she was angry and you'd cross her at your peril.

She stood nearly as tall as Kaneesh and wasn't intimidated by him. But then neither was he by her. He would just listen impassively, letting the torrent of angry words wash over him until her rage had burnt out. Then he would dismiss it all with a gesture, and walk away to a corner of the boat, where he would take his dice out and start to roll them over the deck, as if they would tell him where the next batch of clouds could be found.

But at other times, they would be sitting together laughing, or lazing under the canopy, sharing a bottle of some kind of wine, which they had traded for a few litres of their water.

In the evenings it was usually Kaneesh who cooked the main meal. You could smell the herbs mingling with the simmering rice. They weren't vegetarians, but didn't eat meat. They ate sky-fish though, which Kaneesh had caught. There wasn't much choice when out in the far, empty sky. It was eat sky-fish or eat nothing.

Sky-fish were plentiful out in the Main Drift, but were shy about coming in too near to land. You could always tempt them with a titbit or a morsel on the end of a line though, and then you could catch them in an instant and they would be flailing in the net. I must admit that we ate them too. I hated to see them killed. But they did taste good.

Our main staple is rice. Rice needs a lot of water to grow, and every grain we eat is imported. It is grown on the few islands in the system to have an abundance of water. They form a vast archipelago, over ten thousand kilometres from here. They are often covered in cloud and have huge natural, underground wells. They are called, unsurprisingly, the Rice Islands. Unimaginative maybe, but accurate and apt.

After the Cloud Hunters had eaten their evening meal, Jenine would do her homework and her mother would read or laze or work on the boat, or sometimes she would sing. You could hear her voice carry on the soft, warm air. The songs were always sad somehow, like laments for long ago, for things lost, for people loved and remembered, for everyone and everything which would not come again.

The sound of Carla's singing always made my father smile. He would hear her when he was working late, as her voice echoed and drifted around the harbour.

'Typical Cloud Hunter,' he used to say. 'Only happy when they're miserable.'

But he used to get a faraway look in his eye too, as if he were trying to recapture a moment that had gone, and he always left the office window open so that he could hear every word of the song.

Sometimes, though not often, it would rain on our island. The Cloud Hunters were in temporary trouble when it did, for nobody would buy their water. Why should they, when they could get it for free? The rain might go on for a week and they wouldn't earn a penny. But then it would stop, and that might be it for months on end, and people would again have to rely on the usual sources: the few natural springs, the water-making machinery, and the Cloud Hunters.

A Cloud Hunter in the rain.

It came to be an expression in our house. My father coined it.

'What's the matter with you? You look like a Cloud Hunter in the rain.'

It meant that you looked incurably miserable. And a bit wet.

13

quayside

'Don't forget to bring a sleeping bag and a bedroll,' Jenine reminded me, the morning of our departure. And that was about all the advice I got.

I had just time to get home to change my clothes and to pick up my things. I scribbled a goodbye-see-you-soon note for my parents and hurried down to the port.

The Cloud Hunters' boat was tied up at the quayside, with all eternity beneath it. I walked along the short gang-plank between the deck and the harbour wall. There were no safety rails. When I looked down I saw the vast empti-ness below me and then far, far below, a pattern of distant islands. They seemed as small as the specks that sometimes float in your eyes. Under that was the glare of the sun.

What if I fell? I wondered. If I panicked, lost buoyancy, and couldn't swim my way back up? What if I slipped right now? If I missed my footing?

I looked up to find Kaneesh watching me: a malign smile on his face, as if enjoying my discomfort.

'Hello,' I said. Rather feebly too, I realised. But it was too late to say anything different. I wondered if I ought to spit or something. Or curse a little. Maybe that would impress him. 'I'm – er – Christien,' I explained. 'Jenine said that I could –'

He nodded and indicated that I was to come on board. He didn't offer to help me with anything. His hospitality stopped at a nod.

I went on board and put my bedroll down; he immediately moved it somewhere else. But I think he would have moved my things no matter where I had put them.

Jenine was in one of the cabins. She and her mother appeared after a few, for me, uncomfortable moments in Kaneesh's company. He was stowing supplies for the journey and making a last-minute check of the equipment. I felt that the best way to help him would be to stay out of his way. He probably thought the same.

'Hi, Jenine.'

'Christien – so you came?'

'You thought I wouldn't?'

'Maybe not –'

Jenine seemed pleased enough to see me. I said hello to her mother. Her wrists were heavy with bracelets. She asked if I had everything and I said I did. So she suggested that Jenine show me around while they got ready to cast off.

The boat was quite plain and basic. The bulk of it consisted of storage tanks for the water. The compressor to condense the cloud vapour sat up on the deck; it was compact and reasonably quiet when in use. There was a galley below deck, a couple of cabins, a toilet, a sink, and not much more.

Two kinds of energy powered the boat: wind and solar. The buoyancy of the boat could be adjusted to compensate for its laden or unladen weight, depending on whether the water tanks were full or empty. This control was achieved by varying the power output of the solar panels, or by reeling in, or letting out, the wind sails. Uncovering the solar panels gave the boat more power and lift; closing them reduced that.

The wind sails were there as a bonus, to give extra speed when the breeze was blowing in the right direction, or to use when there was no sun for the solar panels to function.

Yet the boat could travel without wind sails too, even in cloud, just as long as there was power in the back-up storage batteries. The solar panels constantly replenished these. Fully charged, this battery reserve contained enough power for a good five-hundred-kilometre journey, maybe more.

After looking around below, we went back up on deck to cast off and to see the island recede behind us. Kaneesh opened the covers from the solar panels and inched the boat out into the sky. Soon, we were over a kilometre away, and when I leaned over the side rail to look down, I could see faraway islands, at all different levels, and beneath them that haze of eternity.

'Dizzy?' Jenine asked.

I denied it.

'Not especially.'

'Some people get dizzy – the first time. Or they feel a little sky-sick.'

I denied that, too, though the motion of the boat was indeed making me queasy. But I wasn't going to admit it if I didn't have to. I noticed Kaneesh look across at me, as if willing me to be sick, if only for the entertainment value.

'If you do need to throw up,' Jenine advised me, 'try to do it over the side.'

Where else would I have done it? I thought. Where else was there to do it? What did she think I was going to do? Use my shoes?

Her mother went down to fill a flask of water. She returned and offered it to me. I drank some, though I wasn't really thirsty. I thought it might help me feel less nauseous, but it didn't, it made me worse. The motion sickness only went about two hours later, after we'd had something to eat. I was lucky it didn't last all day. Some people have to endure it for a whole voyage.

Soon the island was a long way behind us, as we headed straight out into the open sky. Kaneesh seemed to know where he was going, though there wasn't yet a cloud to be seen anywhere. The air was empty.

The further we sailed from land, the more creatures we saw. Sky-fish constantly passed us, both above and below the boat, or they briefly flew alongside to keep us company.

One blindly flew at high speed into our open sail and ricocheted off like a tennis ball.

'Come on, let's feed them.'

Jenine showed me how to feed the smaller, slower sky-fish, with a little food on the palm of your hand. The sky-minnows would fly right to you and nibble it up. But if you tried to grab them, they'd be gone in an instant. Kaneesh could catch them though. He could pluck them right out of the air. Then he'd hold them a moment, laughing at their wide-eyed helplessness and futile struggles, before flinging them back into space.

Sometimes, at home, I'd buy fresh sky-angel fish from the market just to give them their liberty, to throw them up into the air and to see them go scudding away as fast as they could. There was something rewarding about setting captive things free.

While Kaneesh was busy fishing, I decided, just out of interest, to count his tattoos. I got to twenty and gave up.

14

spare some change

As we sailed on we passed a sky-trawler. It was rolling out a huge purse net, over two kilometres long. It let the net drift in the sky, then slowly tightened the ends, drawing the sides of the purse together, trapping all the sky-fish that had become ensnared.

The trawler hauled the catch along in its wake, towing a great rainbow of sky-fish, of all shapes and sizes, some of them edible, some of them not. There were sky-clowns and sky-angels and even some small sky-sharks entangled in the net, a medley of squirming, panicking, bewildered life. The fishermen didn't bother to haul the catch on board, they just headed for whichever island was home, or for the nearest market, where they could sell their catch.

'Disgusting,' Jenine said, as she watched them go. 'And cruel. Half of them are inedible and die for nothing. They just get thrown away.'

Yet she ate sky-fish herself. But maybe that was different. The Cloud Hunters only caught what they needed, with no wastage and minimal cruelty. Kaneesh killed them in an instant, with one slash of his knife or with a blow from a small stunning implement he gleefully called 'the priest'. Then the head of the fish would be overboard, its innards gutted, and its body filleted and in the pan.

I think you'll eat anything when you're hungry enough, unless your principles are stronger than hunger; and not many people's are when it comes to it.

Carla and Kaneesh left Jenine and me to ourselves. They were too busy conferring over which direction to take, where best to head to find clouds.

Kaneesh stood at the prow, staring into the distance; Carla held the helm to steer the boat. But it was easy enough to lock on course. It could practically sail itself.

Later, Kaneesh went below to start cooking. He reappeared after a while and spoke to Carla, who went down to take over from him. He locked the steering onto automatic pilot, then squatted down on the sun-baked deck, and took out his dice.

I edged over to see what he was doing. He glanced up and gave me a look of annoyance, but he didn't tell me to go away. He cupped the dice in his hands. There were five dice altogether, each with six sides, and each side bearing not a number but a symbol: some kind of indecipherable hieroglyph.

He shook the dice together, let them fall, studied them, left three of them where they were, picked up the remaining two, shook them, threw them down again. He left one of them where it was, picked up the other, shook it in his hand, threw it down. He studied them again. Then he scooped them all up and repeated the entire performance.

Next, he went over to the helm. He adjusted the course by a few degrees and opened up the solar panels, so as to increase our altitude.

Well, if that was how he navigated and located clouds, then I thought it was nothing but meaningless superstition. I didn't see how throwing a few dice around could tell you anything. But he seemed to believe in it, and he was the tracker. It was his responsibility to find the clouds, and he was to blame if we didn't see any.

Yet there had to be some wasted journeys. I knew there were. You could see it in the Cloud Hunters' faces, when the boats limped back into port, as dry and empty as when they had left. Nobody succeeds all of the time. It was like my father said: the person who never failed never tried anything. At least not anything difficult.

I plucked up the nerve to speak to Kaneesh.

'Does throwing the dice find the clouds?' I asked.

'It helps,' he said tersely.

'How?'

'That's our business,' he said. And walked off.

He was a man of few words, was Kaneesh. And not all of them were pleasant ones. No, he wasn't much on conversation.

*　　*　　*

Once we had changed course, I saw a small island appear ahead of us. And as we neared it I realised that it was populated: by a community of one.

'Jenine,' I said. 'Look. A castaway. Or a shipwreck survivor. Hadn't we better stop and pick him up?'

She smiled and shook her head.

'Hermit,' she said. 'And a mad one. We pass him all the time. He doesn't want to be rescued. He wants to be where he is. He likes to be lonely. But he's not above cadging a few supplies.'

Sure enough, as we got nearer to the tiny island, its sole occupant began to act in an eccentric and alarming manner. He rushed to the very edge of the rock and stood there, as if about to lurch off into space.

He couldn't have shaved for years, nor washed for months. You could smell him from a long way off. He and his island stank of rancid sky-fish; and strewn on the shore were dried fish bones and shrivelled sky-weed. Strips of coloured cloth were braided into his matted hair. His few possessions lay on the rocks around him. There wasn't much, just a bed, a few cooking pots, some hooks and lines, a water barrel, and that was about it.

'Alms, brothers!' he called. 'Alms for a saintly man. Or buy a *Big Issue* – a few years out of date, but none the worse for that.'

Kaneesh grinned when the old man called to him. (If he was old. I assumed he was. Perhaps I was mistaken. It was hard to tell. Maybe he was just hairy.)

'You?' Kaneesh shouted back to him. 'Saintly? You might

be more saintly if you washed. It's next to godliness, people tell me.'

'Water, brother,' the hermit answered him. 'A few drops, for pity's sake, to moisten these cracked lips and this shrivelled tongue.'

'And why should anyone pity you?' Kaneesh asked him – though I noticed that he had already moved the wheel and was guiding the boat in. 'Did anyone ask you to maroon yourself on this godforsaken clump of rock in the middle of nowhere? Or wasn't it your own choice?'

'Godforsaken, you say?' the hermit answered. 'Anything but. God's here if he's anywhere, brother, answering his servant's devotions. He's right here on this rock, in all his grace and glory. Water, brother, and I'll say a prayer for you. I'll say one for you all. I have a direct line to things spiritual.'

'Don't delude yourself,' Kaneesh said. 'You don't even have the right number. If I want to say prayers, I can say my own. And to better gods than yours.'

'My prayers can find clouds for you.'

'My wits and dice can find them faster.'

The hermit watched as the boat neared. He could see that Kaneesh intended to stop for a moment, despite his abuse.

'Water, brother, and I'll tell you where the clouds are,' he kept on. 'You're Cloud Hunters, of course. What else would you be? An honourable profession for a hardy race. I can give you help.'

'The day I need your help,' Kaneesh told him, 'is the day I'll give this up for ever.'

'Water, brother, if you've any to spare. I'm parched as a desert, dry as a stone. I've nothing left but a cupful.'

'Then why did you ever come here, to die of thirst?'

'The Lord will provide.'

'You won't need us then.'

'You are the instrument of the Lord's provision, brother.'

'Is that a fact? And what's the Lord up to while we're doing his work for him? Is he having a snooze?' Kaneesh was a heathen all right, and proud of it.

Jenine's mother heard the commotion and came on deck. When she saw who it was she smiled.

'Ah, beautiful lady –' the hermit began.

'Give him some water,' Carla said to Kaneesh. 'How much can we spare?'

'Each drop given is a cloud found, bounteous lady,' the hermit said. 'It's good fortune to give alms to a hungry man.'

'I thought you said you were thirsty,' Kaneesh reminded him.

'That too.'

Kaneesh stopped the ship, right next to the island. The hermit hurried over to us, carrying his empty water barrel. Kaneesh took it from him, filled it up, and returned it. The hermit almost bent double under its weight. Staggering, he placed it down on the rocks.

'Thank you, friends. A million blessings. I'll pray for you now, for clouds and good speed.'

'So which direction, hermit? Where do we sail?'

The hermit stared at Kaneesh, as if he had only just

seen him. He sniffed the air and stared all around, then he raised a gnarled and bony finger and pointed to the far distance.

'There,' he said. 'That way. Even now the clouds are forming. They gather like believers who assemble to hear the prophet.'

Kaneesh nodded, as if he had been looking not so much for direction as for confirmation of the course he had already decided upon.

'Here,' Kaneesh said. 'Make a change from sky-fish.'

He threw the old hermit a small sack of rice and a bag of cakes.

'Gratitude to you, brother. Gratitude and prayers.'

'Maybe you could risk a little wash,' Kaneesh told him.

'The Lord will provide,' the hermit said again. (Though quite what that had to do with washing, I had no idea. Maybe the hermit was waiting for the Lord to provide him with some soap.) 'Blessings upon you, sir,' he said, as the boat moved away. 'And on you, too, kind lady, and on these two young people. Blessings on you all and come visit again.'

'And bring more water, you mean,' Kaneesh grinned.

'Alms to the poor are a blessing to the giver,' the hermit said.

'Well, don't get lonely,' Kaneesh said. He waved and turned the boat back around into the open sky.

'The true hermit is never lonely in the company of his thoughts,' the hermit called after us. 'Solitude is the balm to the soul. Crowds are but noise and confusion. Thoughts and prayers are the best company; thoughts and prayers and contemplation. I'll pray for you all and for peace in the world, that one day all our islands will join together into one great land.'

'I hope not,' Kaneesh said. 'Not in my lifetime.'

We left the hermit behind us. I felt that although Kaneesh laughed at him, he admired him, too, in a way. He admired his madness, his self-imposed isolation, his stubborn, uncompromising individuality. He admired the fact that he had survived all alone on his arid, barren rock.

'How did he ever get there?' I asked Jenine. 'He doesn't even have a sky-boat.'

'He did once,' she said. 'The hermits sail into the middle of nowhere, find an island, load on what they have, then they scuttle their boats and let them fall to the sun. Then they're committed. There's no going back.'

'Don't they ever die?'

'Some do. But then we all die, don't we – in time?'

'Yes,' I had to admit. 'I suppose we do.'

'But then some of them get so many visitors, they're not really hermits at all,' Jenine said. 'People go to them, wanting charms and spells and miracles. They think of them as holy and take them food. You just need to build a reputation for wisdom and holiness, and you're in business.'

I went to the bows of the boat and looked back. The hermit sat greedily drinking a cup of water. Then he went to open the bag of cakes, and that was when I realised he wasn't alone.

One of the rocks came to life.

It was a sky-seal. It had been basking there, huge and immobile, all the time we had been speaking. It was fat and ungainly, and it clambered clumsily over the rocks towards the dishevelled hermit, as if it had designs on his barrel of water and his bag of cakes.

The hermit heard or saw (or, more likely, smelled) it coming. He turned, picked up some stones and pelted the sky-seal with them to make it retreat. The creature hesitated, but not for long. The stones slowed it down but didn't deter it, and it kept on coming. The hermit grabbed a strut of metal which lay on the shore, a remnant of his boat, maybe. He approached fearlessly and began to beat the sky-seal about its rotund body and its disproportionately small, bony head.

The sky-seal emitted terrible grunts and roars, but the hermit went on thumping it until finally it scuttled away to escape the blows and slid off the shore into the sky. It was extraordinary to see such a fat thing fly, but it floated like a pumped-up balloon.

It glided away towards a lower rock, where it would be safe and out of harm's way. The triumphant hermit reached into the bag and took out one of his cakes. He bit into it. He must have seen me watching him, for he waved and he pointed at the far rock with the sky-seal now upon it.

I saw him off, his wave seemed to say. Did you see that? Scrawny hermit defeats fat seal.

And I had to admit that he had. He may have essentially

been a spiritual man, but he was pretty handy with a club.

I waved back enthusiastically, to give him my seal of approval.

'Seal of approval!' I shouted. I felt the joke was too good not to share.

Jenine raised her eyes to heaven.

'Funny,' she said. 'You have any more like that?'

'Plenty,' I told her.

'Yes,' she said. 'That's what I'm afraid of.'

She and I were getting on a whole lot better, I thought. Things were starting to thaw.

15

cloud bank

We were well outside the shadow range of any large islands and there would be no darkness for a while and so, for us, no night. Without a nearby land mass to come between us and the sun, day just continued indefinitely. It was strange to feel tired, to expect the night to fall, but to have the light shine as brightly as ever.

Although everyone gets tired, not everyone gets darkness. Many islands do get night-time, but others are in perpetual day. Our sun is beneath us. But its light illuminates not just the base of the islands, it goes around and is reflected back by the particles in the upper atmosphere. So we usually have light and plenty of it. Our problem is getting hold of the night.

On my home island, we're fortunate. Beneath us is another massive island which passes between us and the sun on a regular cycle. So every day (so to speak) we have night. It's not total darkness, but it's enough. But some islands are out of range of others; they have no satellite island and so have constant light. So people have to make their own darkness, with blinds and canopies and shutters and with thick, heavy curtains to block out the light.

Just as true day and night are more convenient, old-fashioned notions than realities here, so are the seasons. There is no comparable rotation of nature, as in the old world; no annual cycle of spring, summer, autumn and winter. No seasons, no years. There are just the days, cold or sizzling, depending on how far you are from the core. The sun never really rises and never really sets. It just is. We keep the old time system for old times' sake.

But you get used to it. Why wouldn't you, when it's all you've known? You can get used to almost anything.

Occasionally two islands orbit so closely and with such synchronisation that the upper isle permanently blocks out all the light that otherwise would have been reflected back to the lower one, which is then held in constant darkness.

But this doesn't mean such places are uninhabited. They are. But by nothing savoury. These places are the Islands of Night. And most people with any sense (especially a sense of danger) avoid them, like the plague.

We ate our meal as we sailed. Maybe it was dinner, maybe supper; I'd lost track. But it definitely wasn't breakfast. Afterwards, Jenine and I talked for a while as we lay sprawled on the deck. The sky was clear and cloudless and shimmering blue.

Sometimes Carla looked anxiously at Kaneesh, or went to talk to him in a confidential whisper. Now and then they argued, as she questioned his decision to pursue the direction we had taken. But he didn't alter course. We went on heading for wherever we were headed.

I looked at my watch and saw that it was past midnight. I was exhausted but couldn't sleep. Jenine suggested that I go below and use one of the bunks down there. But as nobody else seemed about to do that, neither would I. If they wouldn't sleep, I wouldn't either. I was determined to show them that I meant business, that I could be just as tough and had as much stamina.

At about quarter to one, Kaneesh unfolded a bedroll, shook it out onto the deck, then stretched out upon it. He took the bandana which he habitually wore around his neck, tied it instead around his eyes, and promptly fell asleep.

So I did the same, making a blindfold from one of my spare T-shirts. Jenine slept too. Only Carla stayed awake, to take the first watch.

I was woken at about four in the morning by Kaneesh prodding me in the ribs with his foot. I opened my eyes and glanced up blearily to see him looking down at me.

'Your watch,' he told me. And then, as if by way of explanation, he added, 'No passengers.'

So I had to get up, drag myself to the prow and endeavour to stay alert and watchful while the others slept. I felt tired and irritable and a mite resentful. But I was pleased in a way, too, that I had been asked and expected to take my turn and to do my share. The last thing I wanted was any favours. What I wanted was to be accepted.

I stayed there for two hours, watching shoals of sky-fish drift languidly by. I saw a sky-whale in the far distance, like a cloud itself. But of real clouds there were none.

I had one false sighting and was about to wake everyone, but realised my mistake. It wasn't a cloud at all, at least not of vapour. It was a pillar of insects, hundreds of metres high, moving like a tornado, whirling and spinning as if trying to drill a hole in the air.

The column passed a long way to starboard. Had it hit the boat, we'd have been in trouble. It could have knocked us off course, or worse. Swarms of sky-midges had been known to get into people's mouths and nostrils and down into their lungs. A colony of flying sky-ants could turn a living shark into a dead carcass in minutes – stripping it down to the bone. Islanders lived in terror of these airborne termites. When they came, they threw them meat; while they were busy with it, they sprayed the swarms with chemicals or fire.

At six, Jenine stirred without my waking her and took her turn at the watch. I covered my eyes and slept until eight, when the smell of breakfast woke me. Kaneesh was in the galley. Carla was at the helm, staring into the distance, with binoculars held to her eyes.

I didn't quite hear what she said at first, but I looked up at the sound of her voice when she repeated the command louder and more peremptorily.

'Get Kaneesh,' she said. 'Tell him they're here.'

'What?' I said. 'What are?'

'What do you think?' she said. 'Clouds.'

91

She let me look through the binoculars. They were many kilometres away, some hours' journey from us still. They were shaped like elephants and dragons, like mountains and hills. They changed form as I watched them, like self-sculpting clay – artist and material all in one.

I went down to tell Jenine and Kaneesh.

'Clouds!' I said. 'They're here!'

I couldn't keep the excitement out of my voice.

'How far?' Kaneesh asked. He didn't seem at all surprised. Nor particularly pleased.

'Carla says four hours.'

Kaneesh nodded and went on stirring the pot.

'Good,' he said.

'Aren't you coming up to see?' I asked, feeling that he could have been a little more enthusiastic.

'Breakfast first,' he said.

But then, he'd seen it all before. I suppose he had his priorities and breakfast was nearer the top.

I turned to Jenine.

'Come on deck with me,' I said. 'Please.'

She looked at Kaneesh, as if to ask if he could manage without her. He plainly could and he waved her away. He gave me a look which was half derisory amusement and half contemptuous; then he turned back to his cooking.

It was hard to know what was exciting about it, and yet it was. They were only clouds, after all, not living beings or sentient things. They weren't going to try to run from us, or take it into their heads to escape, or about to turn and attack us. They were only vapour, just moisture, that was all, a haze of mist in the upper sky. But it was exciting, all the same.

We took it in turn with the binoculars. The clouds were large and puffy, white and grey and tinged with pink. They shifted and divided constantly, endlessly restless. They swirled and grew, joined up, separated and changed shape yet again.

'Where do they come from?'

Jenine looked at me the way Kaneesh had looked at me, with the same amusement.

'What are you so excited about? You've seen clouds before.'

'Yes, I have, only . . .'

Only not kilometres from land, never out in the vast, empty sky, with nothing but space above and beneath me, in the company of a girl whose eyes were the colour of green gems and whose beautiful, intriguing face was scarred and disfigured with lines which only made her seem even more beautiful and intriguing – at least to me.

Maybe it wasn't the clouds at all. Maybe it was her. And maybe she knew it.

I handed back the binoculars.

'What makes them form here, and not somewhere else?'

'Updrafts – temperature – humidity. The conditions have to be just right.'

'Will they stay like that?'

'No. Sometimes they vanish before you can reach them.'

'And then?'

'You keep on looking.'

'What if you don't find any?'

'You go home empty.'

'And then? If you've no water to sell? And you don't make any money?'

She looked at me with amusement again.

'You go hungry for a while.'

Was she serious? Nobody went hungry, did they? Not these days. My doubt must have showed.

'Look, Christien,' she said. 'Your parents have jobs, don't they? Work and salary and promotions and insurance and pension schemes.'

'So?'

'They work for sky-traders?'

'My father does, yes. He's an administrator. It's a huge company.'

'What happens if it loses all its ships?'

'That could never happen.'

'Why not?'

'It's a huge fleet – it just couldn't.'

She sat on the rail and raised the binoculars to her eyes.

'Anything can happen. The world lives on danger,' she said. 'We're all insecure, all of us. You think you're stable, but you're not. It's just an illusion. You're standing on clouds, not solid ground. And clouds can melt at any time. You're no more secure than we are. You just don't happen to have realised it yet.'

She turned her gaze towards the cloud bank.

I could see them quite plainly now, even without the binoculars. They went on building, becoming denser and darker grey. Jenine called to her mother.

'They'll rain if we don't get there soon.'

'I know,' Carla said.

'Is that bad?' I asked.

'Of course it is. If they rain, they're gone. Use your head.'

I must have blushed, because Carla laughed.

'Don't take everything so personally, Christien,' she said.

'Can't we go faster?' Jenine asked.

Just as she did, Kaneesh came up from below, carrying a pot of food and some bowls. He handed them around.

'The clouds are thickening,' Carla told him. 'How long, if we go to full speed?'

'Two hours maybe,' he said. 'But it won't be pleasant.'

'Let's do it.'

He shrugged and went over to the selection of levers set into the deck by the helm. He pulled back the guards to open the solar panels, then he told me to come and help him while he unfurled the wind sails. I wasn't a lot of use and he knew it and he should have asked Jenine. But he didn't. I think he just wanted to show her how stupid and impractical I was. Or maybe he really wanted to teach me something. Either way, I learned how to do it, and the next time I'd be able to get it right.

My food was cold by the time I got back to it, but I ate it anyway. We were moving swiftly now, so much so that I had to put on a coat against the chill. The boat bucked and rolled on the thermals, sometimes jumping alarmingly, twenty, thirty, even fifty metres or more up into the air; or it suddenly plunged the same distance down.

95

'Want a life jacket?' Kaneesh asked me.

'I can air-swim,' I told him.

'You can?'

'Of course.'

'In open air? In thermals like these?'

'Well – off the land.'

He threw me a life jacket.

'Put it on,' he said.

I felt a little embarrassed, but saw Jenine put one on too. He was right, anyway, I'd never swum in the air in the presence of thermal currents which could toss you twenty metres in the air or suck you down like a feather into a whirlwind.

The clouds seemed to be retreating, but not as fast as we were gaining on them. The grey of them was turning to black. Then I saw a dark haze falling.

'Rain!' Kaneesh muttered angrily. And he followed that up with what sounded like a lot of swearing in a dialect I didn't understand.

But it didn't rain for long. There were still plenty of clouds left, whole mountain ranges of them, enough to fill the holding tanks to their brims.

My excitement went on mounting, the nearer we got. Everything else was forgotten now, there was just us and the clouds. It was the perfect hunt – at least for me, for it felt thrilling and dangerous; there was the chase and the chance of failure, and to cap it all, nothing got hurt, nothing got killed, nothing died, no living thing was destroyed.

The prize was water, that was all. You didn't have to stab it or kill it or rip it apart. You had only to collect it. Cool, clear, pure water, two parts hydrogen and one part oxygen, a crop of chemicals in its way. The clouds were a herd of giant, peacefully grazing, wool-gathering, virtual sheep.

The vapour went on swirling. The ship cut through the air. Carla's long, braided hair streamed behind her. Kaneesh went to the helm and stood next to her, his hand on the wheel by hers, close enough to touch, but not touching.

'How long now?' she asked.

'Few minutes,' he said. 'I'll check the compressor. Hey, you!' he called in my direction. 'Come here.'

I went with him to check the compression equipment.

'Does that look all right to you?' he asked. The amused expression never left his face.

I nodded. I didn't really know what I was looking at, or looking for. But if he was satisfied, then so was I.

While we were checking the gear, I looked around to see what had happened to Jenine. She was standing by the deck rail, with her hand shielding her eyes, staring at something off to our left. The clouds were straight ahead, so it couldn't have been those. A moment later she turned around and shouted.

'Kaneesh!'

'What?'

'Look at this!'

We looked to port, following her extended arm and pointing finger. Kaneesh cursed again, worse than before.

I heard Carla mutter something too. She looked at Kaneesh and he made a gesture with his hand, as if wishing to put a hex on something or to give it the evil eye.

'What is it?' I asked Jenine. 'I can't see anything. What is it? Where –?'

Wordlessly, she handed me the binoculars. The black speck in the western sky became clear and visible. It was a boat. A boat just like ours.

'It's another Cloud Hunter. Isn't it?'

She took the glasses back and put them to her own eyes. 'Of a kind,' she said.

'Where's it headed?' I asked, rather unnecessarily.

'Where do you think?' she snapped.

Then I realised that it wasn't just a hunt any longer. It was something else as well. It was a race too. A race to be first to the clouds. We were two packs of hunters after the one quarry. And sharing didn't enter into it.

16

cut-throat competition

We watched the other ship as it approached. It was of similar construction to our own, but its water storage tanks were patched and welded, as if recently damaged by a meteor storm. Its hull was pitted and full of dents.

We were almost equidistant from the clouds. The other boat was running flat out, as we were, with its solar panels fully open and its wind sails billowing. It was plainly desperate to get there first.

'Can't we go faster?' Carla asked.

Kaneesh shook his head.

'No. But we have more of the sails.'

He meant we had the wind more directly behind us, which the other boat did not. It was tacking: that is, its sails were catching the wind from an oblique angle, so its speed was less, though perhaps it didn't have quite so far to go.

'Recognise it?' Carla asked him. 'Know them?'

Kaneesh shook his head again. His hands gripped the wheel.

Jenine took the glasses and looked through them, adjusting them to get better focus. Then she lowered them and her face seemed dismayed.

'They're not true Cloud Hunters. They're Barbaroons,' she said.

'Are you sure?'

Her mother took the binoculars and looked for herself. She turned to Kaneesh and nodded.

'She's right.'

Kaneesh swore again. His hand went to the knife in his belt, as if to reassure himself that should it be needed, it was there.

'Barbar-what?' I asked Jenine.

'It's what we call them. It's a general term – a type. It means criminals, pirates, cut-throats. Uncivilised people. No traditions. No culture. People like that.'

'The competition?' I said.

'You could put it that way.'

'So?'

'There's no agreement with them. They're not real Cloud Hunters, not like us. Just opportunists. They'll steal anything.'

'Meaning?'

'It means they'll try to take the clouds, no matter what. First there, or last there, they'll still try to take them.'

'What do we do?' I naively asked.

'We don't let them, of course.'

'But how do we stop them?'

The three of them looked at me, but none of them

answered. If there was any kind of a reply, it came from Kaneesh, who took his knife out, checked the sharpness of the blade with his thumb, and then put it back into his belt.

Cloud Hunters are usually known to each other, and they're mostly of similar ethnic origins. But not all. Anyone who wants to can get a boat, rig it out and take to the skies to hunt for clouds. Which literally would make them a Cloud Hunter. But in practice things are not so straight-forward.

For one thing, there is the question of acceptance. If other Cloud Hunters don't regard you as having a legitimate right to hunt, nor feel that you possess the correct credentials of custom and tradition, then although they will make no attempt to stop you, they will make no effort to assist you either, should you land in trouble. You're not a fellow hunter in their eyes; you're a poacher, a thief.

And, more importantly, they won't play by the rules. They will take the clouds from under your nose, and there won't be a thing you can do about it.

Not that there *are* explicit rules, just unwritten, tacitly agreed forms of conduct which have evolved over the years, in order to minimise conflict.

First: the clouds belong to everyone. When abundant, there can be no quarrel. When there is enough for every-body, then every hunter is entitled to their share.

But when the clouds are meagre and are barely enough to fill one ship's tanks, then the first boat to reach them and to start up the compressors has title to them. Any other ships must withdraw. That had always been the convention and most of the time it was peacefully observed.

But not everybody plays by the rules. Water is water after all. It's worth money. Water pirates were a constant hazard. And now we had some, right in front of us. And the brutal truth is that might is right. There is no real law in the open sky. There are international regulations, certainly, but rarely any authority to uphold them. The laws of the land don't really apply where there is no land for them to apply to. The only people there to look after us were ourselves.

Carla went to the cabin. When she returned, she too had her knife at her waist.

I began to wonder if I shouldn't have stayed at home. And Kaneesh obviously thought the same.

'We should never have brought him,' he mumbled to Carla, thinking himself out of earshot. But I heard.

'He's her friend,' Carla said. 'She's alone too much. He's someone of her age.'

Kaneesh turned his head and spat over the side of the boat.

'Friendship with land-dwellers! Education!' he sneered. 'What good is it? What is she going to learn that she can't learn here? Table manners?'

'Things you'll never know,' Carla said.

'And never need to,' Kaneesh snapped back.

'No, because this is all you'll ever do,' Carla snapped in turn.

'And what will she do?' Kaneesh said, angry and defiant. 'Where will she ever fit in now with those scars on her face? It's too late. She's branded and you know it. An exile, everywhere she goes. An outcast, like the rest of us.'

'Her father wanted it, not me,' Carla said. 'We quarrelled over it. I told him she was far too young – that it was a bad tradition that had outlived its time. It should stop. We should end it.'

'What's done is done. It's too late now and can't be changed,' Kaneesh said. 'She's a Cloud Hunter and always will be. She's as marked as you and me. Where can she go? What island will have her? Everywhere she goes the scars tell the story. She's a Cloud Hunter. They all want water and they look down on those who gather it. They think we're barbarians, but they can't live without us.'

'Prejudice is there to be overcome,' Carla said, her face set like stone now.

'Ha!' Kaneesh didn't seem too impressed by that. 'Listen,' he said. 'No one will ever overlook the scars on her face, any more than they will overlook the tattoos on my arms or the colour of my skin.'

'It's the same colour as mine,' Carla said.

'Exactly.'

'There are a thousand islands with a thousand colours. There's room for everyone.'

'Not for us. We're hunters. Hunters have no homes. Just the journey and the sky. It's in her blood, as it's in yours and mine.'

Carla didn't answer immediately, then she said quietly,

almost as if speaking to herself, 'If, in the future, she met and married a land-dweller – maybe her children –'

I'm a land-dweller, I thought. I'm still young and single. I wonder if . . .

Kaneesh shrugged.

'Maybe . . .' He turned his head around to look at the other boat. 'But who would have her?'

Jenine didn't hear them. She was at the other end of the boat, but I heard every word. I had never much thought of it that way before, that the scars the Cloud Hunters bore on their faces were more than mere ceremony or decoration; they excluded them too, in numerous ways, from any other life. It was self-perpetuating, almost as if there would be no Cloud Hunters if there was no exclusion, no lack of alternative or lack of acceptance elsewhere.

No, you couldn't see someone with scars like that sitting happily and contentedly in some office job, or behind a bank counter. Just the look of them would frighten the customers off. As for the idea of putting Kaneesh in a suit and a tie, you may as well have put a sky-shark in one, for all the naturalness there would be to it. The sky-shark would have been more convincing, and probably more comfortable.

No, even if Kaneesh had given up cloud chasing and become an upstanding member of the Civil Service, he'd still have gone around frightening people with his appearance. One look at that scarred face and you'd have paid your income tax immediately, without even querying the amount.

*   *   *

Jenine turned around. I watched her. Maybe she had heard after all, or perhaps they were telling her nothing that she didn't already know. She looked momentarily sad and she reached up and touched the scars that ran down her face. I tried to imagine her without them; she would have been like anyone then, just another girl – or would she?

Maybe even without them she would still have been different. I knew that I could have picked her out from any crowd, whether her face was scarred or not. There was just, well – something about her. Something unusual, something free. Those green eyes were like jewels.

Perhaps one came with the other: the scars bought the freedom, but the freedom branded you as different, an outcast, destined to travel, to wander, and for ever, in a way, to be excluded and alone. It seems in life that for every plus there is a minus, and that even freedom itself doesn't come free. For that too, there's a price to pay.

'Jenine . . .'

I felt I had to say something – something consoling, reassuring.

'What?'

'The scars . . . I think they make you look – distinguished.' (That was wrong. Inadequate. That wasn't what I'd really meant to say.)

'They make me look like a freak, Christien. And that's what I am, isn't it? An ugly, defaced freak. Isn't that what everyone thinks?'

'No. No. They don't. No.'

'They do. I've heard them.'

'Not me. I don't think that. You look beautiful.'

She stood looking at me, through her green, piercing eyes.

'Christien,' she said simply. 'Don't be ridiculous.'

She went and sat alone at the prow. I let her be. What could I say? How could she believe she was ugly? She was the most beautiful thing I had ever seen.

I joined her after a moment. I glimpsed a flash of sail. The rival boat was running fast, wind sails full out, spinnaker billowing, solar panels yawning wide.

'Tell me about these Barbaroons,' I said. 'Who are they? Where did the word come from?'

It wasn't an expression I knew, but even the most unfamiliar words may have all-too familiar meanings.

Jenine laughed.

'It's a cross,' she said, 'between two words. It's a combination, of barbarians and poltroons.'

'What's a poltroon?'

'I thought you were supposed to be educated.'

'Nobody knows everything. Only the ignorant think that.'

'A poltroon is a trivial person. It's an idiot. A buffoon. Well, Barbaroons are untrustworthy, unpredictable, and usually violent.'

In other words they were criminals, pirates and kidnappers, just as I had thought.

'And what do the Barbaroons call Cloud Hunters?' I asked her.

She either didn't know or preferred not to tell me.

'Why don't you ask them?' she said. 'We'll be close enough soon.'

We were gaining on them – we were maybe two hundred metres ahead, if that. We sailed into the first outlying wisps of cloud. I reached up, trying to touch one. Not that you can. What are clouds, anyway – just water ghosts.

'Hold the wheel.'

Kaneesh left the helm and went to the compressor. We entered the thick of the cloud. He fired up the pump and it spluttered into life.

'There. It's done.'

We were first there to the cloud bank. We had staked our claim. The question was, would they respect it? Would the crew of the other boat turn around now and leave us to collect our water in peace?

The answer to that question came immediately.

And the answer we got was no.

17

drastic remedies

They were quite invisible now, fog bound. The other boat was lost in the cloud. But we could hear the sound of an engine firing, and then the drone of another compressor.

'Hey, you there!' Kaneesh shouted into the mist. 'Turn it off!'

But they did not hear, or chose not to listen, for the drone went on.

I reached out into the cloud again. My hand vanished, and then it came back to me. It must have been as you read in the books about the old world, when someone had their first experience of snow. It was half miraculous and half ridiculous. It made you want to laugh.

Jenine saw me and smiled at my pleasure in what was, to her, such a commonplace, everyday thing.

The other boat remained hidden from us – unseen, but faintly audible, behind the pulsing of our own compressors. They were stealing our clouds – our water. Was Kaneesh going to let them get away with it? He didn't seem the easily forgiving type. Yet neither he nor Carla moved to stop them.

Then Kaneesh did a strange thing. He shut our compressor off. But why? Whatever was he doing? Was he was actually giving up, letting them take it all, handing them the prize? But then I understood that he wanted to track the cloud-hidden boat by following the sound of its engines.

'Over there.'

Carla nodded and steered the boat to starboard. The drone of the other boat's compressor and the sound of its pump grew louder. The cloud became denser; it was so dark and grey around us now that I could barely see the deck. Jenine wavered in and out of sight. One moment she was there, the next she was gone, like an apparition.

I shivered. I felt cold and my clothes were damp. The outer world had gone. All there was now was fog: dense, silent, concealing, muffling the sound of everything like a heavy curtain. Even the throb of the other boat's compressor seemed to come from behind a screen of glass. Then suddenly a dark shape loomed into sight and as quickly vanished.

'There!'

Carla turned the wheel in pursuit of the vanishing shadow.

'Hey, you!' Kaneesh called again.

Nothing. No response. Perhaps they thought that if they ignored us we might go away.

But Kaneesh wasn't the going-away type.

He gestured to Carla to bring the boat around again. As she did, he climbed up onto the deck rail, holding on with one hand to the rigging. The shadow of the other boat reappeared. I could make out the silhouette of three figures on board; they seemed like phantoms.

'Keep her steady!'

Kaneesh took his knife from his belt. He steadied himself on the rail, balanced himself on the balls of his feet, let go of the rigging, then he leapt. He was gone into the cloud and vanished from sight. The fog closed around us again.

Carla held the ship steady. Jenine ran to the side, to that point on the deck from which Kaneesh had jumped. I went to join her. We listened, our hearts the only sounds we could hear, just them and the faint drone of the other boat's compressor, and then –

Voices. Raised in anger. The sound of an argument. I could clearly hear Kaneesh. He was asking the men in the other boat what they thought they were doing – didn't they know the customs and the laws? Then there were other protesting voices, denying his claims, disputing his assertion that we had prior entitlement, that our speed and first arrival had given us precedence.

The quarrel became angrier. There were shouts and threats and the sound of fighting.

Silence again. The boat's compressor had stopped. There was a cry of anguish and dismay. Then once again silence, as the thick cloud swirled around us, leaving me damp and shivering, both with cold and with apprehension.

Kaneesh? What had happened to him? What had he done?

Our boat suddenly shuddered as it collided with the other ship, the bows of which momentarily appeared from the fog. The two boats slid around each other, and as they did, I saw a figure balanced on the other ship's prow. The shape leapt towards us and landed softly on the deck. Immediately, Carla wrenched the wheel around to flick the bows outwards, and the other boat was gone again, drifting away, its compressor silent.

Kaneesh was back, his skin gleaming with moisture, his face grinning. He took his knife, wiped it on his bandana, and put it back into his belt. Carla looked at him questioningly. In response he raised his index finger to his throat and drew it across his Adam's apple in a slicing motion and he smiled. Carla smiled back, as if to congratulate him on a good job well done. Kaneesh walked across the deck and restarted the compressor. That was the only noise there was now. There was no competition. It had been put out of business.

I felt sick. Not sky-sick this time, just plain, ordinary, deep-down sick. I went to the rail and leaned over, longing to see blue sky again and to feel the sun.

They were the barbarians. Them. Kaneesh. Kaneesh had killed the man on the other boat. He had slit his throat, over ownership of a handful of clouds which, in reality, could belong to nobody. Kaneesh had killed him and Carla had approved. Maybe Kaneesh had even slaughtered the whole crew, all three of them, not just the captain. He looked capable of it, without a doubt.

111

I glanced over to where Jenine was standing on the deck, watching the vapour billow into the mouth of the compressor as it sucked the clouds into its lungs, like a smoker inhaling. She also seemed quite unperturbed, as if this were an everyday occurrence. And maybe it was.

I looked at Kaneesh again. He had taken his knife out and was etching a scar into his forearm, the way a gunman might notch a mark on the barrel or the butt of his gun: one mark for every kill.

I turned away. I wished I was home. I wished I had never come. I had known that the skies were lawless, but I hadn't expected this. I wished I could be sick, I tried to retch, but nothing came. I turned away from them all and leaned my head against the coolness of the rail. My hair was damp from the vapour of the cloud. I loathed the lot of them, Jenine included. How could Kaneesh have done that? To kill a man for a tank of water? And for the others to condone it? Maybe my mother had been right after all. Maybe they were savages at heart.

'Christien? What's wrong? You look ill.'

Jenine was by my side. I didn't answer her.

'Hey, what's the matter? You look green. Are you sky-sick?'

I raised my head to look at her. Her eyes seemed genuinely sympathetic, her expression concerned. Her face, like mine, was damp with moisture; droplets of water clung to her braided hair like small, smooth diamonds.

'How could you – how could he?'

'What? What is it? What?'

She was truly mystified, which only served to make it

worse. She was baffled. Kaneesh had just killed a man, slit his throat in a squabble over a few clouds, and he had come back proud of it, looking for approval and congratulation, neither of which were stinted upon. And that was fine. And she wondered what I was upset about.

'How could he do that?'

'What? Who?'

'Kaneesh. What he did.'

'He was protecting us. We have to fight. We need to stand up for ourselves. Or we're finished. If we back down once, we're finished forever.'

'Why couldn't you have shared?'

'It's the custom, the law of the sky. We were first. They were our clouds. They knew they were in the wrong.'

'But to do that?'

'What? What do you mean? What was so bad?'

I drew my forefinger across my throat in dramatic imitation of Kaneesh, simulating the gesture he had made, and all he had conveyed by it.

Jenine looked at me, first perplexed, then slightly offended, and then somewhat amused. She began to laugh. Kaneesh and her mother looked across, wondering what had got into her.

'Honestly, Christien,' she said to me. 'Your imagination's got the better of you. I think you've been reading too many books.'

'You can never read too many books,' I said, sullenly, not liking being laughed at when I didn't know why. What was funny about killing someone?

'Then maybe you could try reading some different ones,' she said. 'Something not so bloodthirsty.' She called across the deck. 'Kaneesh! Come here, come here.'

'I'm busy!' he snarled. Though as far as I could see, the compressor was doing all the work. The only thing he was currently busy with was admiring his new scar and seeing whether it lived up to his old ones.

'No, come here, come here.'

He padded over the deck, like an inquisitive cat.

'What?'

Jenine pointed at me.

'You know what Christien thinks you've done?'

'What?'

Jenine raised her forefinger to her throat and made the slicing motion.

'That's right,' Kaneesh said. 'I did. And what about it?'

'Tell him what you cut,' Jenine said.

'The compressor pipe, of course,' Kaneesh said. 'What else?'

I felt myself go hot with embarrassment. Even in the greyness of the surrounding cloud I was sure my face must be glowing red like a beacon.

'He thinks you cut the captain's throat!' Jenine said. Kaneesh looked at me, an expression of disgust on his face. He shook his head.

'Idiot,' was all he said. Then he padded back across the deck to check on the performance of the compressor.

And that was just how I felt. Like an idiot. A complete one. One who wins prizes for it.

'I can't begin to apologise . . .' I stammered.

'Then don't,' Jenine said.

'Have I upset him?' I asked.

'Not much,' she said. 'I shouldn't think so. He's not easily upset. He's probably pleased that you think he's capable of it.'

'He probably is, isn't he?' I said.

She shrugged in reply, as if to say, What do you imagine?

'Well, I'm sorry anyway,' I said.

'Yes, well, it just shows what you really think of us, doesn't it?'

'No, no, really, no. I didn't think that, I just . . . misunderstood.'

She shrugged again, as if it didn't really matter one way or the other.

'Maybe next time, you'll try to have a higher opinion of us,' she said. 'Give us the benefit of the doubt?'

'I do. I have. I mean, I will,' I said.

'Don't look so serious,' she said. 'I'm only teasing you.'

I didn't know what to say to her half the time. Or I knew what I wanted to say, but was incapable of saying it, as I was too afraid to open my mouth for fear of finding my own foot in it.

She sat down on the deck and patted the space next to her as an invitation for me to sit too. I sank down and squatted by her.

'I can't believe you thought that,' she said. 'Did you really?'

'Well – you know.'

115

'Kaneesh? Slit someone's throat?'

I glanced over towards him. He was sitting on the deck now too, his legs in the lotus position; he was sharpening his knife on a small stone and polishing the blade with a rag.

Yes, I thought, you might smile, Jenine. And you might know him a whole lot better than I do. But I still think he's capable of slitting throats. In fact, it wouldn't surprise me at all to learn that he had slit a few already and was making plans to slit some more at the first opportunity, when nobody was looking. Yes, he looked like quite an experienced and accomplished throat-slitter to me.

I realised that my hand had gone to my own neck and that my fingers were gingerly touching my Adam's apple. Kaneesh looked up at me, and saw me there, with my hand protectively around my throat. He gave me a white-toothed, sardonic smile, and went on whetting his knife.

18

bugs

We hovered there, in the cool, damp mist, with only the sound of the compressor for company. The other boat had long gone. Gradually, the cloud thinned around us, vacuumed from the sky. I could feel the beginnings of warmth permeate through it and make out small patches of blue, which gradually widened, like rips in a piece of cloth.

There was a gurgling sound. Kaneesh turned the compressor off and the world was silent again. There was a slight overspill of water, which washed up on the deck. Kaneesh detached the compressor hose and let the run-off trickle into a cup.

'Well?' Carla asked.

He tasted the water, seemed happy with it and handed her the cup. She passed it on to Jenine, and then it found its way to me. The water was cool and fresh, with a slight, indefinable taste to it, maybe the taste of some mineral, maybe just the taste of the sky. It seemed like a respectable vintage, in my estimation. Not that I was an expert.

It was night once more, by the clock at least, if not by the light. Our water was all collected and it was time to sleep. Carla turned the boat around and set a course for home. As before, we took turn with the watches.

Carla did not sleep on deck, but went below. And then it was my watch. Kaneesh had gone below too. I supposed he wanted to get out of the light and to sleep in some proper darkness.

When Kaneesh took over the watch from me, I lay down in my sleeping bag on the deck. I draped my T-shirt over my eyes, but I couldn't get to sleep. So I took the T-shirt off my face and just lay there, feeling the motion of the boat as it drifted through the sky.

I looked across at Jenine, who lay asleep, half curled into a ball. I felt that I wanted to be nearer to her, and so I wriggled across the deck, moving in my sleeping bag, slithering like some chrysalis – telling myself that a chrysalis was truly a butterfly inside, given the time and opportunity to hatch out.

I was close to her now. So close that I could almost feel her breath. I moved closer still – just to smell the scent of her hair, to see the movement of her eyes behind their closed lids, as she dreamed.

Abruptly, she moved in her sleep, with a sudden violent motion, flailing both arms and legs around, and as she did she caught me an almighty blow across the head with the back of her hand and her knee went into my stomach. I

118

yelped and rubbed my nose and rolled away, clutching at my midriff.

It took a good few minutes for the pain to go. When it finally did, I heard the sound of soft laughter. I raised my head and saw Kaneesh, leaning against the wheel. He had seen everything.

'Ask first, next time,' he chuckled. And he laughed some more, then he turned away, and checked that the boat was on course. Then he looked at me again. 'You know your trouble, boy,' he said. 'You try too hard.'

But as far as I could tell, Jenine was still asleep. I didn't think that she had hit me deliberately.

I lay a while, looking at the sky. Kaneesh moved to the prow of the boat. I slithered nearer to Jenine in my sleeping bag.

'Jenine –'

'Yes?'

'You awake?'

'No. I'm fast asleep.'

'Jenine –'

'What?'

'Do you ever feel lonely?'

She rolled round to face me and opened her eyes.

'Sometimes. Why?'

'Lonely, even though you're not actually alone?'

'Sometimes.'

'Me too.' We were silent a while. Then, 'Are you lonely now?' I asked.

'A bit,' she said.

'We could cuddle up,' I said. 'And then we wouldn't be so lonely. Would we?'

She sighed. 'No, Christien,' she said. 'I guess not.'

'So is that OK then?'

'Yes. That's OK.'

So I got a bit closer and I put my arm around her and she covered my hand with hers. And we fell asleep.

But we didn't sleep for long. When I woke she had gone. All that was left of her was her sleeping bag.

What woke me was a loud succession of violent thumps and bangs, each coming rapidly after the other and causing the whole hull to shake. I experienced the distinct feeling that the boat was dropping down from the sky, losing buoyancy and sinking fast towards the heat beneath us and to the furnace of the sun.

And it was.

'Hey! Boy!'

Kaneesh's big toe dug into my ribs. It seemed to be his principal method of attracting my attention. I yawned and looked up at him.

'What is it?'

He was holding a boat hook.

'Take this and get to work. We've got visitors.'

I stumbled to my feet, still half asleep. I looked around. Jenine was at the helm. Carla was at the rail, leaning over and peering down. She had a crowbar in her hand and was busy using it, trying to prise something off the hull.

'What's going on?'

I got to the rail and looked. My question was immediately answered. Looking up at me was one of the ugliest, most repellent faces I had ever seen. It seemed like an immense bedbug or head louse. I'd viewed pictures of those, taken through microscopes and magnifiers. But no microscopes were needed for these examples. And no picture would ever do them justice.

The face I saw was flaccid and grub-like, with a cascade of chins. It had a sharp, pointed proboscis, like a hammer-drill head, topped by two sets of feelers and two glistening, vacuous eyes. The creature's body was both beetle- and slug-like. It seemed to have more arms and legs than could possibly be needed, while tufts of bristle and ragged hair protruded from its flesh.

'What are they? Sky-riders of some sort? I've never seen them like that before.'

'No,' Kaneesh said. 'They're lice.'

'Where did they come from?'

'Who knows? Off the back of a sky-whale. Anything.'

When you hear of a sky-whale with fleas, you appreciate the fact that you have hands. It is one of the greatest privileges to have arms and hands and the ability to scratch yourself; an itch then turns from an irritation to a luxury. It's a thing you can almost wallow in, the pleasure of a good long scratch.

But to be a sky-whale, out in the air, with a parasitic flea holding on to you and trying to burrow into your skin, with no means of getting rid of it, unless you can find something to rub yourself against, or find a friendly tooth-fish to groom you, is nothing but torture.

When sky-whales grow sick and die, they fall down into the sun. But sometimes they dive there deliberately, to put an end to their misery.

'Those fleas have got wings!' I hadn't expected that.

I saw the translucent wing cases, and the wings beneath them, twitching. The lice were huge, at least a metre tall. If one of them landed on you, or if that proboscis went into you, or if that revolting face with that mouthful of teeth . . .

'Prise them off! They want the water. It's moisture they're after.'

They were trying to drill through the hull and into the tanks. They had proboscises like chisels.

'How do I get them off?'

'Like this.'

Kaneesh took a boat hook, slid it down between the louse and the hull, and wrenched the little monster away. The louse fell for a short distance, then opened its wings, flew back up and reattached itself.

'Or if that doesn't work . . .'

This time he raised the boat hook and aimed for the creature's neck, not to prise, but to stab. The point sank in; the louse shuddered, lost its grip and slid away. This time it didn't come back. Carla was beating at the others with the crowbar in her hand. Jenine was holding the ship steady.

I gingerly looked down and chose a louse to start on.

I hesitantly pushed the boat hook forward. The louse looked up at me and swatted at the shaft with a feeler. I got the hook properly under it and tried to prise it off, but it seemed stuck on with glue.

'Don't play with it!' Kaneesh snarled at me. 'Get rid of it.'

I pulled the hook back up to get some leverage. This time I rammed it down hard, with all my strength.

There was a disgusting noise, nearly as repellent as the louse's appearance. The thing gurgled and looked up at me – almost reproachfully – its antennae twitching violently and its feet scratching desperately to hold on to the hull. It began to fall. It made an awful, high-pitched scream. As it went, it left a streak of blood along the hull. Its blood was yellow.

It took us two exhausting hours to get rid of them. Afterwards the hull remained sticky and glutinous, with patches of slime from where they had latched on. There was a smell of offal and decay in the air, which took a long time to go. It seemed to cling to the boat, travelling with us for hours.

I pumped some water out and washed my hands. As I stood scraping the last of the yellow goo from my fingers, Kaneesh came over and slapped me on the back.

'Good sport, huh!' he said. 'Good sport!'

Well, it might have been his idea of sport, but it wasn't mine.

'The barnacles are even worse,' he added.

Personally, I didn't see how they could be.

'Get a barnacle on your back, that's some fun!'

Kaneesh chuckled to himself at some happy reminiscence of barnacle-bashing. Then he went below to the cabins. At least he didn't seem to dislike me quite as much as he had.

I saw him later, whittling a mark into the mast. It was one of many. There was a whole selection there of five-barred gates: four vertical lines and one diagonal. I asked Jenine what they represented.

'His kills,' she said.

'Of what?'

'Sky-lice. And other things.'

'Does he keep a record of everything he's put an end to?'

'More or less,' she said.

I saw that there were further marks on other parts of the boat. I presumed that they were nothing to do with the mast tally, but represented something else. I didn't ask what they stood for. I really didn't want to know. Maybe it was the barnacles. If so, it was an impressive reckoning. Some barnacles were reputedly as big as a man's torso and it was said that they could crush your rib cage flat.

But I kept thinking of the sky-lice, and of one of them landing on you, and enfolding you in its appalling embrace. I hoped the ones we had killed didn't have friends who would want to avenge them. But maybe lice don't really have friends, just competitors.

'How many of them did you kill?' Jenine asked me.

'Fifteen – maybe twenty. And got rid of a lot more.'

'Not bad. We'll make a Cloud Hunter of you yet,' she said.

She may not have realised – and she may not have meant it – but she said just the right thing.

19

back home

I had forgotten all about the homework until the last moment. We sat on the deck, with home in sight, hurriedly working through the exercises. We finished five minutes before we docked.

As soon as we tied up, Kaneesh went to find one of the water dealers and brought him to the boat, while Jenine and I cleaned and tidied up around the deck.

The water dealer soon arrived, short-legged, over-sized, and very out of breath as he tried to keep up with Kaneesh. He waddled up the gangplank, bowed to Carla, then went and sat down with her while Kaneesh drew off a jug of the water from the tanks. Kaneesh brought the jug over with two cups and set it down on the deck between them.

Carla poured the water out and proffered one of the cups to the dealer. He accepted it. He sniffed it, looked down at it with feigned distaste, then raised it cautiously to his lips. He took a sip, letting the water run around his mouth and over his tongue. He grimaced and finally swallowed.

'Hmm,' he said. 'Well . . .'

'Well?' Carla said. 'How much?'

'Well,' the dealer sighed, 'it's not a lot of use to me, water of this quality. But I dare say I could take it off your hands. Maybe somebody might buy it. It's all right to wash with, I suppose, or bathe in, or to water the plants.'

Kaneesh glared at him. The dealer knew full well that the water was of the finest quality. He just had to try and beat the price down. It was more than a habit with him, it was an instinct.

'If you don't like it,' Kaneesh told the dealer, 'then leave. We'll sell it to someone else. I can find a private buyer, just like that!'

He snapped his fingers under the dealer's nose. The man didn't even blink. He was used to hard bargaining, thrived on it. It was his meat and drink.

'Kaneesh!'

Carla appealed for his patience. Kaneesh walked away and left them to it. Protracted negotiations took place. The water was tasted again. Maybe, the dealer conceded, it didn't seem quite so bad this time. Yes, maybe it was drinkable. Not any kind of vintage, of course, but decent enough.

And so it went on until they agreed on a price. They shook hands and the dealer left. He soon returned, with some of his men and a large, wheeled container. They connected it up to the ship's tanks and drained them out. Then he paid and Kaneesh counted the money – twice – before letting him leave.

It was time for me to go too. I thanked them for taking me with them – the way I'd always been told to do.

'You're welcome, Christien,' Carla said.

'I'll see you tomorrow, I guess,' I said to Jenine.

'Yes,' she said. 'I hope you enjoyed yourself.'

'I did.'

'That's our hospitality returned then.'

'Don't feel you shouldn't invite me again, though,' I said.

'I'll see you tomorrow, Christien.'

I nodded to Kaneesh. He nodded back, just about. Or maybe he didn't. Perhaps it was the motion of the boat which made it look that way. Then I waved one final time and turned for home, my bedroll over one shoulder, my bag over the other.

I walked on by all the familiar sights, past the landmarks and the people I knew. Soon I saw my house and, beyond it, the fine view of the open sky and the distant islands. My mother was tending her small herb garden. In her hand was a can of water, spray dribbling from the spout. You had to be well off to afford a garden and a pool, even one only half full of water. My father was sitting reading the newspapers, a drink in his hand. He looked up and saw me and he waved, then he called to my mother.

I felt that I didn't belong to them or to this place quite as much as I had. I had gone where they had never been, already seen sights they had never witnessed. I suppose that's how it happens: little by little you grow up; little by little, you detach yourself from the old familiar things.

Then one day you realise that you have let them go completely, and they no longer have a hold on you either. Not as they once did. You are like two hands, still reaching out for each other, but your fingers no longer quite touch. You have let each other slip; you have to let go.

'Did you have a nice time, dear?' my mother asked. 'Nice weekend? With your . . .' She hesitated, wondering what to call them, and finally settled on, ' . . . friends?'

I told her that it had been all very nice, very interesting and highly educational. I stressed the educational aspects. My father was listening and seemed both doubtful and amused.

'And you did all your homework?'

'Of course.'

'Good.'

I wanted to tell them right then and there that I had made a great decision; that I now knew what I wanted to do with my life, what I wanted to be. I knew how I intended to spend my adult years and days, until my time had all run out.

I want to be a Cloud Hunter, when I grow up and leave home . . .

But it sounded too childish, even to me. It was the *when I grow up* part that did it.

I want to be a Cloud Hunter . . . one day . . . soon . . .

So I didn't say anything, not then. I decided not to tell them for a while. For I could picture my mother's face clouding over with dismay and disappointment, and my father, wry and indulgent, saying, 'Oh, give the lad his head for a while. He'll soon grow out of it.' As if he knew all the ways of the world, and that my dreams were just a passing phase on the road to some greater maturity.

No, I'd keep my goal to myself, and slowly work towards it. And one day I would go. I'd sail out into the vast blue sky in search of the great grey and white clouds. And this time – this time – I'd go and I'd never come back.

The long end-of-term holiday was six weeks ahead. But the time which preceded it seemed longer than any holiday ever could. There I was, and there were my grand designs, and we had been intercepted by eternity. The great obstacle of time had come between us. Time is a barrier nobody can transcend; it is a wall nobody can climb over. And if anyone has invented a way to make it go faster, I've yet to see it.

I wanted to go again, with Jenine, with her mother, Carla, and the heathen-looking Kaneesh, with his dice and knives and his tallies of what he'd killed, carved in five-barred notches all up his arms and around the boat. Not just for a few days this time, but on some long, splendid voyage, all the way to the other side of the Main Drift, to the Isles of Dissent, the Forbidden Isles, and far beyond.

The problem was, would they want me? Or, failing to want me, would they be willing to put up with me and take me along? And if they were, or could be persuaded to, what about my parents? We usually went for two weeks' vacation on a luxury sky-cruiser. It was so much of a habit that it had all but turned into an obligation.

I could imagine my mother's face, a picture of perplexity and hurt, when I announced that I didn't want to go this year, that I would prefer to spend the time with disreputable Cloud Hunters, sleeping on a bedroll on deck and prising fat sky-lice off the hull with a sharp boat hook.

I dropped hints, small ones at first. I muttered about 'growing up now' and 'doing something different this year, maybe with some friends perhaps', and of 'going away on my own'.

My father, as ever, peered over the top of his newspaper at me, with benevolent scepticism, as though the fact of my trying to establish some independence was a source of endless amusement to him. Or maybe it was the battle between myself and my mother which kept him entertained. I think he regarded himself as some sort of a referee, the kind who occasionally gets embroiled in the fight and trodden on by the contestants.

Every hint I dropped my mother resolutely refused to pick up. Whenever I expressed the opinion that it would be nice to do something on my own, she countered with how pleasant it was for 'the family to be together'. And my father went on trying to remain aloof from these domestic disturbances. He watched the battles like an observer up on the hills.

I suspected that, if anything, he was on my side, but he couldn't or wouldn't come down on it, for he didn't want my mother to feel that he was ganging up with me against her. As a result, he would never commit himself. Whenever she appealed for his support and said, 'Don't you think?', he would yes-and-no and hum-and-ha about it all, until she got so exasperated she would give up on him and start back on me again.

But if there was one thing I shared with my mother, it was determination and stubbornness. If the Cloud Hunters would have me, then I was going to go with them again. Even if I had to slip away in the night, leaving a note on the kitchen table saying, 'See you when I get back,' and with no immediate forwarding address or contact telephone number.

If they would have me, of course, that was. If.

I couldn't truthfully say that Jenine was conspicuously friendlier after that weekend away than she had been before it. At least not in front of other people. But maybe she was a little warmer if we were ever together on our own.

Sometimes I would look at myself in the mirror and try to imagine my face with the deep, long scars running from my cheekbones down to my jaws, and envisage my arms banded with tattoos, circling like dark bracelets around them.

I could picture my mother's horror if I ever came home looking like that. I could hear her – Oh no! Christien! What have you done to yourself! Followed by the crash of scattering furniture as she passed out. I'd have to be a Cloud Hunter then. There wouldn't be anything else for it. No other career would be open.

Some people believe that your destiny is written in your face, or in the lines of your hands. Well, if that was true for anyone, it was true for the Cloud Hunters. Their scars wrote their futures for them, every page, line and word of the book.

I had only once seen someone with those facial scars doing anything other than hunting clouds. She was a clerk in one of my father's offices. How, or why, she had given up the hunt, I didn't know. But there she sat, in a corner of the office, filling in requisitions and compiling cargo lists, looking like a sky-fish which no longer had the air to swim in, trapped and cooped and unhappy: a wild but imprisoned thing.

She left one day, quite suddenly. She married a settler and they went off to scrape a living on a small, barren island they had bought together. There are thousands of such islands, cheap to get but hard to live on. Still, at least there was nobody there to stare at her scars. Sometimes the only way to be fully accepted is to be with people just like you, or to be alone – another hermit on another rock.

The scars on the Cloud Hunters' faces just draw your eye to them, despite your best endeavours to be polite and not to stare. It's rude to stare, of course, yet you can't help but look sometimes and wonder at the difference between you and them. Maybe there isn't one, not inside, but the outside makes you think so. The scars come between you. You can't pretend that you don't see them, or that they aren't there.

Usually, I suppose, everyone has somewhere, some land

to call their own. But there are always a few people who have nowhere, the dispossessed, and the Cloud Hunters were among them. They had their boats, but as far as dry, solid land went, there was nowhere in the world they called home. They only thing that was really theirs was the sky. And what is the sky? Just empty air. And who can possess that? Nobody owns the sky. Quite the opposite. If anything, the sky owns us all. We are just its citizens. But the sky is the kingdom.

20

free lunch

One day, about three weeks before term was due to end, it rained sky-fish.

A huge shoal was passing, accompanied by the usual attendant predators and opportunists: sky-sharks and sky-fins and all the rest. The fish dropped out of the sky all day long, dead or dying from fatigue.

You just needed to hold your hand out and one would fall into it. Or you could leave an empty cooking pot outside and it would be full by the time you returned home. Some of the fish even fell down through skylights, or smashed solar panels, or they landed in water butts, and drowned.

These sky-fish 'invasions' happened occasionally. The fish weren't always edible either; they might be diseased, or had been swimming non-stop for days on end and were exhausted and scrawny.

All the dead and fallen fish had to be gathered up and disposed of before they started to rot. I went out into the garden after school to help pick them up. They were clammy and cold. Their eyes stared glassily and their wings were folded.

If you opened the wings up, they were like elongated fins, translucent and iridescently shimmering. It was a shame that the sky-fish had died, but we had to get rid of them, or the smell of decomposition would have been awful. Nothing smells good when it's a few days dead.

Once, when I was out in our garden, I thought the sky was bleeding. I was kicking a ball around when I felt a spot of moisture drop onto the back of my hand. I glanced up, but the sky was clear, with not a cloud anywhere.

I looked at the drop again and saw that it was red. Further drops were falling all around me. I shielded my eyes and looked directly upwards. High, far above me, two sky-sharks were visible in silhouette, fighting to the death. They fought for hours, two great entangling and threshing shadows. They were still fighting when I went in to go to bed.

In the morning the body of one of them lay in the garden. My mother rang the council and they came and took it away.

There are tales of children being snatched from the streets, lifted from bicycles or taken from their prams, by hungry sky-sharks. But it always happened to the family of a friend of a friend and no one I ever knew. They're just stories to scare you with.

Throughout the following weeks, I waged a campaign on two fronts, and continued to drop large and conspicuous hints in places where people could not help but trip over them.

I kept asking Jenine what her intentions were for the long vacation, though I knew perfectly well already that she, her mother and Kaneesh were committed to taking water to the Isles of Dissent.

I observed that an extra pair of hands would be sure to come in handy on a long trip like that, and that I knew of a good, available pair, which might be willing to work for nothing.

Jenine never said much by way of direct encouragement, just smiled, as if she knew perfectly well what I was up to, which she doubtlessly did. But I hoped she might pass the information on to her mother.

At home, meanwhile, I diligently kept up the other half of the campaign. I regularly mentioned wanting to 'do something different this year'. I complained that the annual family holiday was all well and good but that there wasn't much to do for 'someone of my age' on a cruise ship filled with 'little kids and old fogies'.

I rubbed away like sandpaper. My mother seemed immune to persuasion, but my father was more sympathetic, saying, 'Well, if he's not going to enjoy it . . .' and, 'If he'd rather be with people his own age . . .'

Then one day I was able to come back and announce that I had been 'invited away for a couple of weeks in the holiday'. Which was quite untrue, of course. I hadn't been invited anywhere, but I'd screwed up my courage and had finally asked to go along.

Jenine and her mother had agreed to my going and had basically conceded that they might be prepared to put up with me for a while. Whether Kaneesh felt the same was doubtful. But there was only one of him. Which was just as well.

In the end my parents agreed that I could go. Our ultimate destination, the Isles of Dissent, did not worry my father so much as which route the Cloud Hunters proposed taking to get there. He spoke to Jenine's mother and she assured him that we would be avoiding anything hazardous and would be giving trouble a very wide berth.

At least that was the intention. But the nature of intentions is such that even the best of them can make paving stones for the road to hell; and to other equally hot and unpleasant places.

I was pleased, but apprehensive. So often, when you get what you want, you immediately begin to think, Do I, did I, really want it? Being tenacious has its value. But you can end up fighting on a point of principle, only to discover, if and when you win, that it wasn't just the principle that motivated you, it was the pleasure of the fight as well.

But I was pleased to think that I could only be going because Jenine wanted my company. If she had told her mother that she didn't want me there, then that would have been the end of it. Or that was what I imagined. And why not? For what sort of a sad, useless life is it if you can't even dream? For dreams don't cost anything and they don't usually hurt anyone, except, perhaps, the people who dream them.

*　　*　　*

As I waited impatiently for the weeks, and then the final days, to pass to the end of term, the boat went to and from the harbour the same as ever.

Sometimes Carla and Kaneesh came back with the tanks empty, but usually the water dealer could be seen making his way to their ship shortly after it had docked. He always walked with the air of a man who could take it or leave it. Yet he never dawdled either, in case someone else got there first. A good dealer must feign indifference, but do so at reasonable speed.

Every few months we would see the huge water fleets of the United Isles pass by. This great archipelago has a land mass of millions of square kilometres, and is enormously wealthy and powerful. Not that we are part of it. Our island is independent, and named Sovereign Isle. Not because we have any royalty. Just because of the shape of the island, which is like a huge, flat coin, with hills and rocks on it; and, when seen from a distance, it resembles the profile of someone's head.

The United Isles never bought from Cloud Hunters. Their water fleets ranged for vast distances, comprising massive sky-ships: long, flat vessels with enormous storage capacity. They flew the flag of the United Isles and had their hulls painted in their national colours. The water they collected was for their sole use. They rarely sold it on.

The fleets would lumber along like great juggernauts, so immense they even dwarfed the pods of sky-whales which passed alongside them, swooping under their bows, or even nudging against them, sending shudders through the vessels, as the whales endeavoured to scratch their itchy backs on the bulwarks to rid themselves of their fleas.

Once in a while, a caravan of nomadic traders would pass overhead. They travelled together in long convoys of numerous sky-boats, propelled by wind and sun, or towed along by harnessed and muzzled sky-sharks.

The great caravans could take days to pass, or they might decide to stop and to hover offshore, so that people could go out in their own boats to see what the merchants had to sell, and to haggle with them over terms and prices. Sometimes the nomads organised races and would send their half-tamed sky-fins streaking across the sky, with riders on their backs. My father claimed that the races were fixed and he would never bet on them. But plenty of other people were ready to gamble and some won a fortune. Or, more likely, lost one.

But finally – finally – the school term was over. The holiday was upon us, and the long trip to the distant and intriguing Isles of Dissent was to begin.

21

departure

We left in the morning. The earliness of the hour and coolness of the air seemed to rob my departure of much of its occasion.

My parents had risen early to be there to say goodbye and we sat bleary-eyed and half awake at the breakfast table. It hardly felt like an apt moment for affectionate farewells; it seemed more like a time for going back to bed and pulling the covers up over your ears.

My father offered me a lift to the quayside, but I told him that I would walk. I said an affectionate goodbye to them both, graciously accepting the money (some for spending, some for emergencies) which I had been hoping that they would offer me. Then I picked up my things and left.

I called goodbye again as I walked along the path. They stood at the door, waving, and looking somehow frail and vulnerable and suddenly older. Maybe it was because they were still in their dressing gowns; maybe it was because people always look older and more fragile in the early morning. I unexpectedly felt that I would miss them – a pang of homesickness before I had even left home.

'See you in few weeks, Christien!'

'Enjoy yourself!'

'And . . .' (I knew what she was going to say) '. . . be careful.'

Why is it that your parents are forever urging you to be careful? As if being reckless, getting yourself killed, or ending up in hospital are all you have in mind? Do they imagine that you have no other plans than to do yourself an injury as quickly as you can? And even if you were careless by nature, did telling anyone to be careful ever make them so?

I had my doubts.

'Be careful, Christien. Remember!'

'I will, Mother!' I called back. 'I will!'

I was hardly going to say, 'I won't!'

The dockside was busy, despite the hour; sailors and fishermen rise early. A couple of sky-trawlers were preparing to set out and their crewmen were checking the nets. Hovering offshore a container vessel, belonging to my father's company, was waiting to come in. It was flat-bottomed, with barely any displacement; rectangular containers sat piled upon its deck like neatly stacked building bricks.

Jenine saw me coming and called hello. Carla waved. Kaneesh looked up from his preparations and acknowledged my presence with a half-friendly scowl. I said hello to him anyway, if only for annoyance value. Everything appeared to have been secured for a lengthy voyage. There were plenty of supplies on board, and there was always water.

I assumed the route that Carla and Kaneesh had plotted would take us to the Isles of Dissent by way of the Outlying Settlements. It was not the most direct, but it avoided the worst of the Forbidden Isles, giving them a good, wide berth.

The Forbidden Isles comprised more than the few I have already mentioned. Almost every month a new quarrel would flare up and a breakaway sect would move away to colonise somewhere uninhabited. It seemed that some people just couldn't get enough of making their own lives as difficult and miserable as possible.

There were other dangerous islands in the system too, but by reason of their beauty, not their occupants. The Seductive Isles were exactly that: fragrant and enticing, wafting the most intoxicating perfumes out from their shores to lure travellers in to land. They seemed like paradise islands, little gardens of Eden.

But the perfumes came from poisonous lichen that covered the rocks. Sailors had been known to abandon their ships, ignoring commands to stay put, and had sky-swum with deft, determined strokes to those lush, scented shores.

Within minutes of setting foot on them, they were dying, covered in that same lichen and soon to be buried under it, turned into human pot-pourri.

There were even tales of an island with flying beings upon it: bird-men and bird-women, humans who had evolved wings. It was false, of course. But maybe one day, ten million years from now, who knows? It might come true.

It was five to seven days' travelling to the Isles of Dissent, and the same back, plus an allowance of four days for loading and unloading and for finding clouds. Normally, the ship arrived with full tanks at the Isles of Dissent, decanted the water, then went back out, filled up again, and returned a few times.

Of course, what I did not know at that point was that this voyage was not merely one to hunt clouds and collect water. That was but part of it. And a minor, almost insignificant and secondary, part too. The real purpose of the voyage went beyond anything I had been told or could imagine. The concealed purpose was one of rescue, with the added possibility of revenge, and murder, and even death.

And the reason I had been permitted to come along was not simply because I was wanted or needed as a sociable companion, but because four pairs of hands were better, in such circumstances, than three. One pair of hands to hold the ship steady; three pairs of hands to rescue – and, if necessary, to kill.

But on that morning of departure none of this was known to me, nor to any of the bystanders or the idlers or the farewell-wavers on the dockside.

Yet they knew: Jenine and Carla and Kaneesh. And no doubt they should have told me the truth in advance of our going, and not simply have revealed it when it was too late to turn back. But I don't really blame them. Not then, nor since. How could anyone who had heard their story?

But the fact was that far from steering a course to avoid the worst of the Forbidden Isles, the Forbidden Isles was precisely to where we were headed.

We were headed to the most perilous and monstrous of them all: the Forbidden Isle of Quenant. This was a place where there was but one dire, dread punishment for all offences, and where it was particularly easy to give offence a hundred times over, without meaning to at all.

But for now, however, I was happily ignorant of all this. And when, as we were leaving, my parents hurriedly appeared at the dockside, having disregarded my request not to indulge in any overdone, last-minute farewells, I waved and called goodbye to them and to all those gathered on the quay.

It always seems remarkable to me, the way people are so ready to wave a fond goodbye, even to a stranger. Mothers hold tiny children in their arms, encouraging them to wave to the departing boats, to the fishermen, the traders, the embarking cruise liners, the catchers of clouds. It is almost an instinct, a spontaneous moment of empathy with a traveller.

It seems that, for all our faults, we still have an inner yearning to wish each other well. I think we want the best for each other, despite it all. We want each other's journeys to be safe and successful. If only out of superstition. Because then our journeys will be successful too. The well-wisher will be wished well in his turn. It's a little bit like touching wood.

We untied the mooring ropes and drifted away on a light, sail-ruffling breeze. Those who were waving to us gradually turned from life-sized people into small specks on what – elsewhere – might have been a far horizon. But there is no real horizon here, just endless, indeterminate distance, and a haze of blue filled with trembling heat.

Soon the island I called home was a speck as well. And we were swallowed up by the vastness, travelling through that azure, eternal sky. We were timeless and endless, beginning-less and unreal. It didn't even feel that we were human any more. We were like clouds ourselves – ethereal, indefinable, insubstantial, just vapour and breath, vague shifting shapes, sprung into life from someone's imagination.

But whose? The imagination of some creator? Or had we imagined him as well as ourselves?

I looked ahead to the distance and wondered about the supernatural and the spiritual and whether any of it was true. And if so, which version was the correct one, out of all the many faiths? Or were all creeds equally valid, equally true, equally questionable, and, ultimately, equally unprovable?

All I saw was sky. A sky without answers. Beautiful, endless sky. And I could hear the breeze fill up the sails and make music in the rigging. And there Jenine was, standing next to me. And I felt as if I had left an old life behind me now, and that a new one was just beginning.

22

garbage ship

The first few days were easy and slow. There was little do and so that was what we did – very little, and with close attention to detail. Doing nothing is a sort of art, and you need plenty of time to perfect it.

For most of that part of the journey, Kaneesh lounged on deck, baking in the sun. Occasionally he shifted himself to trail a line over the side and reel in a couple of sky-fish. Then, when our meal was over, he would gather up the bowls and push them in my direction, indicating that here, at least, was one field of endeavour in which I could make myself useful.

When the washing-up was finished there were usually a few basic chores to do, if only to pass the time: little jobs of maintenance and repair, keeping the boat in order, applying a lick of paint here and there.

I had brought a few books with me, and so had Jenine – schoolbooks, some of them – and we went through them together, testing each other's knowledge of theories and facts. I tried to get her to teach me a few words of her language, but it was hard and guttural and difficult to pronounce.

'How long till we get there?' I asked Kaneesh one long, sultry afternoon.

But he just looked at me as if to say, Where's there? What kind of a place is that? There's only here. Didn't you know?

It was as if here and there were all the same to him and he was already where he wanted to be. And all he wanted to do was to be. And where he did that didn't bother him, just as long as he was.

'A day or so,' Carla said, answering for him. 'Depending on the clouds. We have to fill the tanks first. Once that's done, we'll head for the Isles of Dissent to sell them the water. And after that . . .'

Her voice trailed away. She turned her eyes towards the sight of a massive sky-walrus, perched on a tiny island little bigger than a boulder. The animal looked both sad and comical, with its long tusks and droopy moustache and a melancholy expression, as if it hadn't eaten in a long while.

Seeing it, Jenine picked up one of the leftover sky-fish that Kaneesh had caught and hurled it skywards. The great lumbering creature leapt off its perch and dived after the plummeting fish. It caught it then flew back to its rock and sat chewing. It didn't look any happier though. It seemed just as melancholy as before.

'You're welcome!' Jenine called.

By way of reply the sky-walrus emitted a huge burp and I caught the stench of old fish on its breath.

'Disgusting!'

I fanned the smell away.

'It doesn't have much else to eat,' Jenine pointed out.

Which was true enough. But it didn't make it smell any better.

'Fresh-breath mints,' I said. 'That's what it needs.'

I got a smile out of her. I was getting more of those, as time went by.

Some hours later a battered old barge passed us, its holds and deck heaped high with rubbish. An odour of food leftovers, stale dustbins and septic tanks wafted in our direction.

'Look,' Jenine said. 'Garbage ship.'

I looked through the telescope. The sparse crew were all wearing face masks and protective suits.

'Where's it going?'

'Looks too full to be collecting. Must be dumping. Heading for one the Garbage Islands.'

Which did exactly as said on the discarded tin. These were uninhabited islands populated only by junk. Some varieties of garbage were dumped overboard into the sky to burn up. But other kinds wouldn't always sink, or might fall onto other islands on the way down. So the bulk of our rubbish had to be disposed of by other means. Remote islands were the answer.

There were several island dumps around by now, great

rubbish tips in the sky, half a kilometre deep in trash and debris. When they began to overflow, another island was found. Presumably, in a few thousand years, every island in the sector would be a rubbish island. But nobody worried about that for the present. That was a problem for somebody else.

Later that day we sailed into a floating bloom of vegetation, a field of sky-flowers, stretching away into the open air. The plants grew wild, lightweight and borne on the wind, brilliant yellow and dazzling green, undulating like waves. There were shoals of sky-fish devouring them. The flowers were said to taste like mustard and cress, but I'd never tried them. They were considered a delicacy.

We drifted through them, the boat brushing them aside. Then they closed again behind us. You could reach out and take the flowers in your hand. They tasted clean and crisp, and a little peppery, and they stained your mouth yellow. Jenine laughed at me. She said I looked like a clown. But her own lips were yellow and made her seem even more like an exotic alien. But then, maybe we're all aliens. Maybe we're all just passing through, just visiting. And we all really belong somewhere else.

'So how are we travelling there?' I asked Carla later that evening. 'To the Isles of Dissent? Which route are we taking?'

We'd studied geography and navigation at school. You have to be able to read a sky-chart if you ever want to travel independently. It's not an abstract, theoretical thing; it's an essential, practical subject.

Kaneesh looked up at my question and exchanged a glance with Carla.

'We'll decide on the precise route in a while,' she said. 'Once we've found some clouds.'

But I wanted to show off my knowledge.

'Well, I suppose there are only two ways we can go,' I said. 'There's the trade route along the Main Drift and past the Outlying Settlements, or the more direct route through the Islands of Night. But as that's supposed to be too dangerous for anything other than armed convoys, I guess the Main Drift it is. The only ships that go the Islands of Night way are pirates, smugglers, criminals on the run, and people up to no good. Right?'

But maybe I had said the wrong thing. For none of them answered me. Then, at length, Kaneesh looked up from the piece of wood he was carving and laconically added, 'Or Cloud Hunters.'

I didn't immediately understand his implication.

'Sorry?'

Jenine answered for him.

'Or Cloud Hunters,' she repeated. 'You missed them off your list. They also use that route through the Islands of Night. Along with the all the other people "up to no good".'

'Hang on,' I said. 'I didn't mean –'

Kaneesh's knife went whistling across the deck and embedded itself in the centre of that small target he had carved into the mast. He allowed himself a thin smile of satisfaction. Then he uncoiled from where he sat, unravelling like a piece of rope, and loped across the deck to retrieve the knife.

But they were being evasive, I thought. We still hadn't established the route we were taking. They hadn't answered my question.

'But the Islands of Night route,' I persisted, 'is supposed to be quite treacherous, isn't it?'

Kaneesh pulled his knife from the mast.

'Naturally,' he said. 'What else would it be?'

If anything, he appeared to take considerable delight in the prospect of treachery. He rotated his knife so that the blade caught the sun, and he angled the light to shine in my eyes.

'Hey!'

I raised my hand.

'Kaneesh!' Jenine said. 'Leave him alone.'

He chuckled and put the knife away.

The Islands of Night, I thought. Was that the direction we were taking? If so, then they hadn't really been straight with me, for they hadn't said so beforehand. If my parents had known, they might never have let me go along.

The route past the Islands of Night was favoured by the brave, the foolish, people in a hurry, criminals on the run, and, of course (need it be said?) Cloud Hunters. They were known haunts of renegades, robbers and skywaymen, and reprobates of all description.

Such few explorers as, in the past, had managed to return from the Islands of Night brought stories with them, of pale, white creatures, huge and slug-like, with sightless eyes or no eyes at all. They brought samples of the indigenous plants back too: bleached and colourless, with long, pallid tendrils, which were said to float in the darkness, their fronds stretching out towards you like beseeching hands.

As for the travellers who didn't come back, who can know or imagine what they encountered, or what prevented them from returning? Or maybe you can imagine. But would you want to? You might give yourself bad dreams.

I looked at Jenine. She appeared embarrassed.

'We've done it before,' she said to me later, trying to be reassuring. 'It doesn't take that long and it saves you days of travelling. It's not that dangerous. People exaggerate it. We've never had any trouble – well, nothing serious. Anyway, you're not afraid of the dark, are you?'

'No,' I said. And I wasn't.

I wasn't afraid of the dark at all.

I was afraid of the things that lived in it.

'Honestly, we'll be fine, Christien,' she said. 'And it'll be an experience. Which is what you said you wanted. Wasn't it?'

'Yes,' I agreed. 'I guess it was.'

And she was right in her way. It was an experience. Just not the kind that you want to repeat in a hurry.

23

no accident

On our third day out, we saw clouds.

And you didn't need a psychic, hawk-eyed, lookout (with a sixth sense, five dice and divine intuition) to find these ones either. They simply appeared, assembling themselves around us. Soon they were half blocking out the light.

'Clouds coming!' I yelled. Kaneesh looked at me as if I were a complete irrelevancy, whose only discernible talent in life was for stating the obvious in an unnecessarily loud voice.

We didn't bother with breakfast that morning. We got straight to work. Carla took the wheel and steered the ship while Jenine and I helped Kaneesh to get the compressor ready and quickly checked the tanks and hoses for leaks.

Soon we were deep in fog. After a time we could hear the pulse of another compressor from somewhere nearby, probably another Cloud Hunter. But we never saw them, and Kaneesh didn't bother to challenge them. There was plenty for everyone this time round. The other hunters came and went as we did, like grey ghosts in a grey night.

It took a few hours to fill the tanks. By the time it was done, we were cold and soaked through, and the tanks were full to overflowing. You could feel the weight of them in the altered motion and heavier handling of the boat.

Once the tanks had reached capacity, Carla navigated our way out of the cloud bank into clearer, warmer air. We soon dried off and we felt elated. For the tanks were replenished and we were rich in resources. We had something to sell. We were traders. Water in the hold was money in the bank.

'What's for breakfast?' I asked Kaneesh.

'How about, just for a change,' he said, 'we have some sky-fish?'

'Sounds fine by me,' I said.

'Then you can help catch them.'

Kaneesh threw a couple of lines over the side. As we fished, a flat, wide sky-ray came past, half gliding, half flying. It skimmed the air like a disk. Its flapping wings made a hollow beating sound. I noticed there was a small wound on its side, a cut, still wet with blood. A few minutes later, a sky-shark came along, heading in the same direction, as if in leisurely and confident pursuit, sure that it would get its prey before the day was out. The sky-ray was a dead fish flying.

As the boat was heavier now, our progress was slower, but still steady. Soon I could make out a dark shape ahead

– unmistakably different from everything around it. It seemed to draw in all the surrounding light, sucking the life and energy from it. There were two immense land masses, one beneath the other, and between them was a long, black hole – a tunnel, a kind of living, sentient darkness, a death that feasted on life.

I joined Jenine by the rail; she stood with her elbows leaning upon it and her face cupped in her hands.

'So that's the Islands of Night?'

'Yes,' she said. 'That's them. And that's the corridor.'

'Have you sailed it many times?'

'A few.'

I hesitated to ask my next question. It was a sensitive issue and bound to upset her. But that didn't mean that it couldn't be talked about. Maybe she wanted – even needed – to speak about it.

'Is that where the accident happened?' I asked.

She looked at me, puzzled.

'What accident?'

'The accident – when your father . . . was killed?'

She straightened up and looked at me, her eyes cold.

'Who told you that?'

'I don't know. Someone did. Someone at school. Somebody said. I don't remember. It might even have been one of the teachers. The day before you came. She said there's a new pupil joining, from a family of Cloud Hunters, a girl, and we had to go easy on you –'

'Easy! You think I need any special treatment? I can't stand up for myself?'

'It wasn't me who said it. I'm just repeating what I was told.'

'Easy! Huh! It's me who had to go easy! On all of you.'

'OK, Jenine, but I was only saying. Anyway, I'm sorry – sorry about your father. The teacher said there was an accident – that he was swept overboard by a thermal storm –'

We stood in silence. She seemed offended and to be debating with herself whether to forgive me or not. She must have decided that I hadn't tried to be insulting deliberately.

'It wasn't an accident,' she said finally.

'What?'

'It wasn't an accident,' she repeated. 'There was no accident. And he isn't dead – at least not yet. Though he soon may be. What you heard was untrue. Nothing like that at all.'

I stared at her.

'Then what happened? And what do you mean by "not yet"?'

'He's not dead,' she said again. 'He's a prisoner. Under threat of execution. We've tried every legal means to free him and they've all been useless. We've a stay of execution but no one will implement or uphold it. He'll be hanged in eight days' time.'

'But – who by? Where? How? I mean – what are you going to do?'

'We're going to rescue him,' Jenine said. 'And you can help us. Or, at least, I hope you will.'

'I am? But how? That is, when you say rescue him

– where from? I mean, what happens if you fail – if you get caught?'

'Well, naturally, if we get caught, they'll kill us too, won't they?'

Oddly, for a second, the statement seemed extremely reasonable. Of course they would. They'd kill us. Quite obviously. Who wouldn't?

'So we'd better not get caught, then,' she said. And she turned away and stared at the approaching darkness that was the Islands of Night. Then she looked at me again. 'But I'll tell you this, Christien,' she said, 'if they do execute him before we get there – then we'll have to kill a few of them. And then we'll be even. Won't we?'

Yes, I thought, I guess we will. If you say so, Jenine. If you say that's how it is. Yes, that seems perfectly sensible. We'll kill a few people. What else would we do? But then the full implications of what she had just told me sank into my brain.

Rescue her father? From execution? And if we failed, we were going to kill his executioners? Or die in the attempt? That was it? Apparently it was. That seemed, more or less, to sum it up.

But nobody had told me anything about this beforehand. I'd just come along for the ride. I'd just thought we were going to sell some water and see some sights. I hadn't been planning on rescuing anybody or getting myself killed.

I wondered if there hadn't been a small misunderstanding somewhere along the way. Somehow, somebody had got their lines crossed.

24

quenant

'It was not quite one turning ago. And once every half turning we carry water to the Isles of Dissent,' Jenine continued. 'To two of them in particular, to Freedom Isle and Hippy Isle. Sometimes to some of the smaller ones as well.'

There were scores, possibly even hundreds, of islands in that sector.

Jenine was staring out at the sky. We were alone in it now. There wasn't another boat anywhere in sight. To our left a shoal of sky-fish swam level with our sails – ten or twenty thousand of them. The leading fish suddenly veered away, and the rest of the shoal followed, as if they were all of one body and one mind, a single organism with ten thousand parts.

She turned her attention back to me.

'We went to many of the Isles of Dissent over the years,' she said. 'The Forbidden Islanders won't trade with the Dissenters. They'd let them all die of thirst if they could.

And they would die, too, if it wasn't for us. Cloud Hunters and Dissenters have a lot in common.'

Kaneesh and Carla were watching us from the other side of the boat. But when I looked in their direction, they turned away.

'The Dissenters mostly live by hydroponics,' Jenine continued. 'They grow fruit and vegetables in greenhouses. So their need for water is high. Most islands have their own extractors and condensers. But they still need to buy-in water. They can never make enough. Clouds are few and far between in that region and often blown away by the prevailing winds.

'The Dissenters also make artefacts that they trade at island markets, selling or bartering them for whatever they need. Some of the things the Dissenters believe in are quite sensible; others are quite mad –'

'Such as?' I had to ask.

'You ever heard of people who believe that God is a jellyfish?'

'Well, no – but I've heard of other things just as improbable.'

'Look – there's one there!' Jenine pointed. 'Divinity in person.'

In the distance, a medium-sized sky-jelly drifted by. But it didn't look particularly divine. Just a bit rubbery.

'Anyway, they're the weird ones. Others are more sensible. You get free thinkers and Quakers, pacifists, hippies, pagans, witches, animists, all sorts – you name it.'

'And?'

160

'Well, obviously the Forbidden Islanders next door don't like them. They don't even like each other. And they didn't like us selling water to Dissenters.'

'They'd try to stop you?'

'They have done. Or tried to warn us off. They'd send a gunboat, while we were collecting water. Just to be intimidating. But we'd ignore or outmanoeuvre them or lose them in the clouds. They'd get bored after a while and go.'

'But –' I said. 'What's the but?'

'How do you know there's a but?'

'There's always a but,' I said.

For, even in my limited experience, there usually was.

'Well,' she said, 'that was how it was. But none of the Forbidden Islanders actually attacked us. And as we never docked at any of their harbours, we were relatively safe.'

'But then . . . ?'

'But then . . .'

Her voice trailed away as we watched the sky-jelly float by. I could see its veins; they looked like threads.

I waited for her to pick up the story.

'But then . . . one trip . . . our last big voyage . . . we had trouble. Our solar engine failed. We couldn't fix it and needed spares. There was so little breeze, the wind sails were useless. We had no choice than to drift with the thermals. And as luck had it, they carried us to the Forbidden Isles. And we put ashore at the very worst of them.'

'Which one?'

'The Isle of Quenant.'

'What do they believe in there?'

'I can tell you what they don't believe in.'

'What?'

'Making allowances for other people. The Quenant – the people have the same name as the island – don't like Dissenters at all. Not in any shape or form. They loathe them. All Dissenters are deemed to be heretics. And the Quenant penalty for heresy is death.'

'Death?'

'By hanging.'

I swallowed.

'We're not going anywhere near there, are we?' I asked.

Jenine looked into my eyes.

'Yes,' she said. 'That's exactly where we have to go.'

'H-how near?' I said. 'How near do you mean?'

'Near enough to land there. Because that's where my father is. Rotting in jail.'

'But why do they hang people? What for?'

'They do it in imitation.'

'Imitation of who? Of what?'

'Of the founder of their religion, who was himself put to death, only by some other bunch of intolerant bigots. He was hanged, and after his death, he was revered by his followers as a holy martyr. The Quenant adopted his means of execution as a religious symbol. It's everywhere you go, all over the island. There are nooses hanging all over the place, small and large, in chapels and shrines. And whenever you enter a holy building, or give, or ask, for a blessing, you make the sign of the noose.'

162

'The sign of the noose? What's that?'

She showed me.

'Like this,' she said. 'More or less.'

I tried it for myself. It felt an uncomfortable and sinister gesture to be making.

'So what else?' I said, keen to find out as much as she knew.

'The Forbidden Isle of Quenant is a ghastly place,' Jenine said. 'Even as you sail in, the first thing that you see on a hill above the dockside is a huge gibbet, a gallows. It's massive, with a great noose suspended from it, waving in the wind. One moment it almost seems to be beckoning to you, inviting you to draw near; the next, it seems to be warning you to keep your distance and to stay away.'

'Horrible,' I said. 'What a gruesome symbol.'

She was thoughtful for a moment. Then,

'Hmm . . . yes . . . maybe. That was what I felt at first. But is it though?' she said.

'What do you mean?'

'Well, you look at some of the other religions, the old established ones. They often have symbols like that too. Look at Christianity. Look at the cross. Is that such an attractive image? A poor man being crucified? Isn't that a bit gruesome?'

'But that's different!' I protested. My own parents were Christians. Not that they were exactly regular church-goers.

'Is it though?' she said. 'Is it so different? Then how?'

I didn't want to argue with her, so I just shrugged and let her go on.

'Now the law on the Isle of Quenant is that any stranger who sets actual foot on the place is obliged to adopt their religion. You can tie up by the dockside, you can stay onboard your boat, people can come and trade with you, and that's all right. But if you ever step off your boat, walk along the jetty and then put one foot onto their land, you can be seized and made to convert.'

'And if you don't convert? Or won't?'

'Then you're regarded as denying the Quenant religion. And it's heresy to do that. And the penalty is –'

'Yes,' I said. 'I think you told me.'

And, for some strange reason, my collar felt suddenly tight around my neck.

'Are you all right, Christien?' Jenine asked. 'You look pale.'

'I'm fine,' I said. 'So what happened next? When you docked at Quenant harbour? Did your father go on land? If so, what made him risk it?'

'Get me a cup of water,' she said. 'And I'll tell you.'

25

capture

We drank some water, and she resumed the story.

'So there was a problem with our boat and we had to dock at the Isle of Quenant. That was the island the thermals carried us to. We had no choice. We tied up at the jetty and hadn't been there long before some officials came striding along the pontoon and invited themselves on board. My father explained to them what had happened and that we needed to repair the boat.'

'And?'

'They said that was fine; that they would send someone to trade with us so that we could buy what we needed.'

'And?'

'That was what we did. They kept their word.'

'So why –'

'Just be patient, will you, Christien? Stop interrupting and let me get on with the story.'

'Sorry.'

'OK. Now. We got the parts we wanted and we paid

for them with water. We fixed up the solar engines and we were ready to sail. It was shortly before we were due to leave when it happened. It was early morning, towards the end of the sleeping time. The quay was deserted. We were preparing to cast off when we heard this noise and commotion.'

'What was it?'

'It was a man. We'd seen him before, and he was a nasty-looking piece of work. He was dragging a dog along by a length of rope. The dog was trying to dig its feet in to stay put and it was plainly terrified. It was barking and whimpering all the way. But the man kept pulling it along. He brought it to a gibbet by the dockside – part of a shrine where the Quenant sailors prayed before setting off on a journey. He threw the free end of the dog's lead over the gibbet, pulled hard on it, and yanked the dog up by its neck.'

'He did what! Why?'

'It was a sacrifice, I suppose. An offering to heaven. He was sacrificing the dog.'

'So what did you do?'

'My father leapt from the boat. He ran up the jetty and onto the shore. He struck the man down and freed the dog. But as he was untying the lead, the man shouted for others to come to his aid. He was yelling at the top of his voice: "Heathen on land! Heathen on land!"'

'What did you do?'

'There was just my mother and me. Kaneesh wasn't with us then. We ran to help my father. But he shouted at us to stay on board, or we would be taken too. There were men coming from everywhere, almost as if they had been hiding, ready and lying in wait for this to happen, almost as if –'

'The whole thing had been arranged?'

'Yes, as if the whole business with the dog had been put up, a staged event to get one of us to come off the boat and go to its defence.'

I remembered Jenine and the small puppy, that time when the sky-jellies had drifted over our school and how she had risked her life to save it. I wondered if she had done so because she had seen her father act in the same way. Maybe it had been done in his honour. Maybe she just hated to see suffering. Or maybe it was simply that nothing inspires people more than living example.

'So then?' I said. 'What next?'

'They overpowered him. He's strong, but he was just one against many. They seized him, tied his arms, and put – they put a noose around his neck – and led him away.'

'And?'

'We didn't know what to do. We were afraid to leave the sanctuary of the boat and equally afraid to leave the island. We couldn't abandon him and yet we dared not set foot on the dockside. People came and gathered at the end of the jetty, as if waiting for us to step on to their land, so that they could take us too.'

'So what did you do?'

'We waited. Waited and waited. For hours and hours. Riddled with fear and dread and indecision. Finally a man came to see us. He was dressed differently to the others and looked important. He wore an ornately woven necklace around his throat, which on closer inspection turned out to be another noose. He said he was a priest. He said that my father would be tried the next morning and given the chance to convert to their religion –'

'Or?'

'Or he would be hanged in due course. On Quenant's Day.'

'And?'

'He refused to convert, of course. As we knew he would.'

'So did they –?'

'Not yet. He's still imprisoned. They had a trial, of sorts. They like to put on a display of legality to disguise the fact that they're intolerant bigots. But the verdict's always guilty. Then they hang all their prisoners at their great annual festival. They like to make a big celebration of it. And that's on Quenant's Day. Of course, as it takes place but once a turning, that means you could be on death row for as little as a day or for long as a full twelve dividings.'

'So what did you do?'

'Everything we could. But it's all been useless. The Quenant don't recognise any law but their own. They don't admit to any higher authority than their saviour and redeemer, Quenant himself. So even though inter-island law bans them from carrying out the sentence, that makes not the slightest difference.'

'So you went to the courts?'

'We went to the International Court and got judgement

against them. But so what? What use is judgement without enforcement? And the inter-island authorities don't have the resources. They've got millions of kilometres of sky, and tens of thousands of islands, to patrol. They've got all sorts of trouble on their plate – piracy, smuggling, contraband, trafficking. They don't care about the life of one Cloud Hunter. They've got bigger things to worry about. We're an irrelevance, a speck of dust. And the politicians don't care either. There are no votes to be had in saving Cloud Hunters from a noose.'

I didn't ask her for more details of that day. Nor did she give any. Yet now that I knew the outline of what had happened, I could imagine the rest clearly enough.

We sat on the deck; the breeze was in her hair; her green eyes were dark and thoughtful. After a while she looked at me again.

'So now we have to go back,' she said. 'There's just a short time left.'

'Until?'

'Quenant's Day. When they'll hang him. If we don't free him first.'

I wondered what I had got myself into.

'And if you can't? Or if you fail?'

'Then, if that isn't possible, then we find the man responsible for having him arrested.'

'And?'

'We kill him,' she said simply. 'What else? If we can't have my father back, then we'll have revenge.'

'But you can't do that,' I said. 'You can't kill him.'

She looked at me, baffled.

'Why not? It's the right thing to do.'

'No, it's wrong,' I said. 'You know . . . an eye for an eye . . .'

She still looked perplexed.

'What do you mean? An eye for an eye?'

'An eye for an eye and soon the whole world is blind.'

'Meaning?'

'You shouldn't take revenge.'

'So I should let you blind me but do nothing about it? Is that what you mean? Lie down, roll over? We should turn the other cheek, should we? To be struck in the face again? And again? How many blows and insults is someone supposed to take before they fight back, Christien? What if it was your father?'

'All right, then what if you do rescue your father? You're not still going to kill the man then?'

'Maybe not. We'll have to see. The chance may not come our way.'

'You should seek redress in the law.'

'But it was the law. Their law. Quenant law. Weren't you listening? It was the law of their island. Anyone can make up laws or give the name of laws to injustices. So now this is our law. We're tired of your law, Christien. We exhausted it. The law's no good. The only real law is what you can do for yourself. The police aren't going to risk their necks to rescue my father. They'll leave him to rot. Are you telling me that if someone captured or killed your father you wouldn't avenge him?'

170

'I'm not saying that. I'm not saying I wouldn't do anything. But your father isn't dead yet. I'm just saying –'

'What? That you'd write a strongly worded letter of complaint, would you?' she said with cutting sarcasm. 'Is that what you'd do? Is that how they handle things in your nice, polite world? "Dear Sir," do they say, "I wish to express my strongest objections to your hanging dogs and killing the people who try to save them. Please don't let it happen again. Yours sincerely . . ." Is that how you put things right?'

I kept silent. It wouldn't have mattered what I said now, because anything I did say was just going to make things worse. If her short fuse got any shorter there'd be a major explosion.

Finally I thought of something neutral and non-inflammatory to say, a question which wouldn't make her angry.

'So who,' I asked, 'is Kaneesh?'

'My uncle,' she said. 'My father's brother. He's going to help us to rescue him – or to do whatever else is necessary,' she added. Her voice trailed away.

'And me?' I said.

'You?'

'Yes. Me. What am I going to do? Why am I here, Jenine?'

'You wanted to come. You asked to be here,' she answered, with disingenuous simplicity. 'You wanted to know what it meant to be a Cloud Hunter, and now you're finding out.'

'Jenine . . . why did you agree to my coming along?'

'All right. We're hoping that you might help us too. Help with the rescue . . . and anything else that might need to be done.'

'But I might not want to do that, to help with your rescue or your revenge. I might not want anything to do with it.'

'We just need you to stay and look after the ship. That's all. You don't have to go on land.'

'Don't you think,' I said, 'that you should have asked me and told me all this beforehand? And have explained to me in advance what I was letting myself in for? Instead of leaving it until it's too late for me to get off your boat? What if I want to turn around and go back home?'

'OK, Christien,' she said. 'If you're afraid –'

'I'm not afraid, I just –' But then I corrected myself. Why lie about it? 'OK, Jenine, I am afraid. What's wrong with that? Aren't you? Why should I pretend I'm not afraid when I am? Fear's nothing to be ashamed of. I'm human and it's a human emotion. We can't help it. So yes, I am scared and that's the truth. And at least I'm not too proud or stupid to admit it. Aren't you afraid?'

'Yes,' she said. 'But what can I do? He's my father. Of course I'm scared. But we can help each other to be brave, can't we?'

I didn't reply.

'Look, Christien,' she said, 'we're not going to make you do anything you don't want to. If you don't want to come all the way to Quenant with us, that's fine. We'll let

172

you off at the next populated island. You can call your father from there and he can come and get you. Or you can catch a sky-bus home. I just thought you wanted an adventure, that was all.'

'Yes, I did. But –'

'Always a but, eh?'

'But I wasn't expecting . . . to . . . kill anyone . . . or get killed myself.'

'With luck, it won't be either. And if there is any killing to be done, we'll do it. You can just watch. Or, rather, look the other way. How's that?'

The long, black tresses of her hair blew back from her face in the breeze. She moved away to the other side of the boat, leaving me there staring out at the wisps of clouds and wondering what I had got myself into.

I thought of something I had read in a book once. It said that there are two tragedies in life: the first is not getting what you want; the second is when you do get it. I'd always wondered what that meant. But I was beginning to understand it now.

She called across the deck to me.

'Well then, Christien?' she said. 'Do you want to be dropped off at the next island? Or do you want to make the rest of the journey with us? I'd like you to stay. But you don't have to. It's our quarrel. Not yours. We'd under-stand. I wouldn't think any the less of you.'

'No,' I said. 'I'll stay. I'll stay.'

I answered her without even thinking. And then I did think. Long and hard. I thought to myself that I must be

173

mad. But it felt like a pleasurable madness. And I wasn't going to change my mind.

I stayed because she said she wanted me to. For that, and for no other reason.

26

dive

The strange thing was, after an hour or two, how little it bothered me: that prospect of what lay ahead. After all, everybody lives under some precariously dangling sword or other; they just don't realise it most of the time.

Accident, illness, death, disaster: such threats hang over us every second of the day. Yet mostly we behave as if they didn't exist or we cultivate enough indifference to them to carry on regardless.

It was a long way to the Forbidden Isles, I told myself. We hadn't got there yet and might never arrive. We still had to pass by the Islands of Night. Perhaps we wouldn't survive even that leg of the journey.

So why worry about being hanged by the intolerant Quenant, when we might get eaten by sky-sharks first? Why worry about one particular unpleasantness, when there were so many others that could precede it? No. If you were going to worry about all the bad things that could happen, you'd never enjoy any of the good ones that sometimes did.

I wondered who would be sad about me, if I did die. My parents, of course; a few school friends; Jenine, maybe, if she were still alive herself. I'd maybe get a nice headstone in the memorial gardens. We don't bury anyone here; there are no graveyards. Everyone and everything just turns to ashes in the end. The sun gives life and it's to the sun that we return. The sun is heat, light and existence, and also death and darkness, cemetery and oblivion. It is where we bury our dead. Clean fire. No rot. No decay. Just the long journey down, to where the air ends, to that great, inextinguishable, all-consuming furnace. First the remembrance ceremony, then we set sail, with the body wrapped in a winding sheet, and we lower it over the side, and let it fall.

So no graves, just headstones in the gardens of remembrance; only our memories, and memories of memories. And as long as there is one person left alive to remember, we all live on. At least that's what we believe.

Near our house is a Field of Remembrance, on the headland overlooking the void. Some names here are of the first pioneers – the ones who came from an overcrowded, polluted, war-ridden, dying Earth – their names and their dates and their unfamiliar birthplaces, along with quotations from old poems.

While I was lazing on deck thinking about this, Kaneesh came over and stood looking down at me. As usual he had his knife in his belt and he was rattling his dice in his hand. He seemed friendly for a change, chatty even – for him.

'Hey, boy . . .'

I squinted up at him. He grinned at me.

'So you want to be a Cloud Hunter?'

'Maybe,' I said. 'One day.'

Behind him I saw Carla get to her feet.

'Well,' Kaneesh said. 'If you want to be a Cloud Hunter, then you should look like a Cloud Hunter. And to look like a Cloud Hunter . . .'

He took his knife from his belt and he pointed with the tip of it to the deep scars on his face running down from eye to mouth.

'Kaneesh . . .'

Carla was level with him, ready if necessary to try to take the knife. But he just laughed at her – or, more probably, at me.

'Only offering,' he said. 'Only offering to do the boy a small favour.'

And he returned to the wheelhouse to check our bearings and to alter course a little. Then he began to whistle, as if he didn't have a care in the world, as if he hadn't just offered to do some minor surgical alterations to my face with his sharp, and probably very unhygienic, knife.

He hadn't mentioned an anaesthetic either.

I think he just had a weird sense of humour.

Another stint of steady sailing took us closer to that darkness which we had first glimpsed some kilometres before.

'How long till we're there?' Jenine asked her mother.

'Three, four hours,' she said.

'Is there time to swim?'

Carla motioned to Kaneesh to close the solar panels and slow the ship.

'A short one,' she said.

Jenine walked over to me and kicked the sole of my shoe.

'Hey, lazy,' she said. 'You coming for a sky-swim?'

I got to my feet.

'Sure.'

But when I took one look over the side of the boat, I was petrified. It was a very, very long way down.

I hadn't done a lot of swimming in the open air, not without a safety net under me. The public swimming area off the rocks at home was one thing. But that was the shallows compared to this. This was deep, wide air, an ocean of sky. Lose your buoyancy here and you'd never recover. You'd only stop falling when you were a cinder.

'Ready?' she asked.

She had climbed up to the top of the rail and was poised, about to dive.

'If you are,' I said.

Without another word, she sprang like a fired arrow, arcing gracefully into the air, and then falling down into the abyss.

Then she suddenly levelled, and she was floating on her back, looking up at me, laughing.

'Well?' she said. 'Aren't you coming in? The air's lovely. I felt so cooped up on deck. It's lovely to stretch. Or have you changed your mind?'

Kaneesh and Carla were watching. I couldn't embarrass myself any more than I already had.

'Come on then, if you're coming. We don't have long.'

I decided not to risk a dive. I tentatively lowered myself over the side, clinging onto the rope ladder.

'Just let go of it. Let go and swim. It's the same as water. Just let go.'

I let go.

I thought I was going to die. Or throw up. But I didn't do either. I floated like a cloud.

We didn't swim for long. The air density makes it just possible not to sink. But the feeling is always there, in the pit of your stomach, that the bubble of what you are doing is about to burst, and then you'll zoom around, like a punctured balloon, before falling limply to your death.

Air-swimming is like tightrope-walking. What keeps you up there is a certain degree of skill, a certain amount of faith, and a large (and probably misplaced) quantity of self-confidence. You must never face the reality that your skill, faith and confidence are probably all delusions. Do that and you're finished.

After ten minutes we returned to the boat. Kaneesh uncovered the solar panels. We took up speed again and sailed on towards the Islands of Night. Beyond them I could see tall, spreading plumes of smoke and fire. I asked Jenine what they were.

'The Fire Islands,' she said. 'They've burned and smouldered for years.'

'Why don't they burn out?' I said.

'They will, one day, I suppose.'

But for now they went on burning, glowing orange and

red amid the black and grey smoke. They looked like demons' eyes.

Night.

Too often here, it doesn't exist. So it is somehow exciting to find it. And between the Islands of Night there is real blackness and deep, impenetrable shadow: permanent nightfall.

These islands stretch for over a thousand kilometres. One island hovers above the other, and the darkness is sandwiched between them, like the filling in a cake.

Our route lay not lengthways, but in traversing their widths at the narrowest crossing point. So our journey through darkness was nearer to three hundred than a thousand kilometres. But it was still a long, dangerous way.

We were fifteen or twenty minutes away from entering that black tunnel when Kaneesh, leaving Carla to steer, disappeared down into one of the cabins.

Jenine and I sat at the prow, watching the approaching dusk. We appeared to be sailing into the open maws of some great monster, whose jaws were made from two huge chunks of land. The darkness gaped at us; it even seemed to grin invitingly, in a macabre and baleful way.

Come into my parlour, said the spider to the fly.

Kaneesh came back up from below carrying waterproofs. He threw one set in my direction and handed another to Jenine.

'Put it on,' he said. 'You'll be cold.'

He was right. As we approached the dark, the temperature

dropped. The chill of cold, and the chill of apprehension, entered into you simultaneously, one seeming to trigger off, and to feed on, the other.

Soon we were levelling with the two great islands: one above us, one beneath. Each cast a giant shadow upon the other, creating that tunnel of night. The islands were reputedly unstable too, like dormant volcanoes, and due, at some point, to collapse, one upon the other; it might be tomorrow; it might not be for another million years. The fact that the jaws could close upon you at any moment merely added, of course, to your travelling enjoyment.

We entered the darkness. I looked back. The light behind us was quickly fading. I felt a moment of blindness and panic. But gradually my eyes became accustomed to the dark and I saw that it was not quite as absolute as it had first appeared.

Kaneesh turned on the ship's navigation lights, along with a powerful spotlight, mounted on the bows. There was ample power in the solar batteries, more than enough to take us through the darkness and back out into the light.

First the chill and the dark. Then, when you had adjusted to that, the next thing you noticed was the silence. We sailed on into it. It flowed all around us, above and beneath, running like the silent water of a silent stream.

After fifteen minutes it was nearly as dark behind us as it was ahead. There was just the pale glow of the light we had left, of the lost, open sky, glowing as a faint candle in a room full of night, a pinhole in a box.

The silence was heavy and contagious; the lack of sound made you almost afraid to break it. It seemed as if we were in church, a vast cathedral, where mute, invisible monks were at their solemn devotions, worshipping unseen gods of darkness and tranquillity, and where it would have been blasphemy to speak.

Kaneesh broke the silence. Yet even he kept his voice low, and his tone, if not reverential, was at least respectful of this eerie, alien place.

'Over there . . .'

We looked up. A pale, flaccid creature of bloated appearance, half the size of our ship, wafted out of the darkness and floated effortlessly, weightlessly past us, barely flicking its fins.

'What a disgusting . . .'

It peered at us through tiny, purblind eyes, as if eyes were not things it really needed here in the darkness that was its element; for it had a dozen other, more useful senses, that helped it to get around and to survive.

'What is it?'

'Sky-slug,' Jenine said. 'We'll see plenty more of them.'

As she spoke, the creature's mouth fell slackly open to reveal plates of baleen, like a whale's. It was a filter feeder. It scooped up tiny creatures as it went along, insects and sky-minnows and anything that didn't need chewing. It swallowed them whole. Its mouth looked big enough to swallow any one of us too, and I was glad when it had gone by. I didn't want to be eaten by some big tea strainer.

The creatures that evolved to live in darkness must be among the ugliest in creation. Arguably, when no one can see you, it doesn't matter what you look like. Though that still wouldn't explain why ugliness ever took precedence over beauty, even in the dark. All because no one can see you, that's no reason to look ghastly. It's not as if it costs more money to be nicer looking, and it surely can't be more of an effort.

But then, maybe we're the ugly ones, all of us out here in the light. We just think we're better looking, but we're not. It's only what we're used to. Maybe we're the monsters. It's all, as people say, in the eye of the beholder. And if sight is not one of your senses, then the apprehension of beauty must lie elsewhere, in forms other than visual ones: in scent, in sound, in touch.

Either way, whatever the evolutionary truth of it, we saw some of the ugliest and most grotesque things float by us as we sailed between the Islands of Night. There were things that looked like living gargoyles and things that must surely have escaped from experimental laboratories. There were creatures that appeared to have been made inside out, or the wrong way round, with their innards where their outsides should have been. They were nightmares incarnate: your worst dreams made real.

'Pretty, eh?' Jenine said, as one of these mutations went past. It swivelled its head towards us at the sound of her voice, showing an eyeless face and scale-covered skin. It opened its mouth, emitted a high-pitched shriek of terror, and sped off. I was glad to see that it found us as frightening and repulsive as we found it.

At least that meant it would keep its distance.

I found Jenine's hand in the darkness, and I held onto it, tight.

27

dark lives

The further into the dark we travelled, the more numerous the creatures became. Some were all but transparent. Many were sightless. But some had huge eyes, the size of plates, hungry for any available light. And those night creatures all seemed to be predators, living in a state of constant warfare, preying on the next in line along the food chain.

I saw one animal swim into our spotlight and it was as clear as crystal. Inside it was another creature, which had taken up residence in its innards. Either that or it was lunch. Who was eating whom was quite impossible to determine. Maybe they were simultaneously eating each other, and neither quite knew yet who was the diner and who was the meal.

'What is *that*?'

'Parasite,' Kaneesh said. 'This place is full of them. Everywhere's full of them.'

I got that impression that Kaneesh didn't really hold a very high opinion of the local wildlife.

He stood at the prow, a boat hook in his hand. Now and again he prodded and jabbed at any creatures that ventured too close.

Usually a prod was enough to repel them. Once it wasn't. So he stuck the point of the hook right into a passing sky-slug. It squealed and scurried off, oozing some substance that looked too black to be blood, but who knew?

'How long until we're through and out the other side?' I asked.

'Another eight hours or so,' Jenine said.

I was cold. I sat on a pile of rope and blew into my hands. I didn't much like the darkness. There was a smell, too, of damp and weed and salt; it was fetid and malodorous, as if things were decaying all around us.

The spotlight picked out a tangle of creepers ahead. It was impossible to see if they grew downwards from above or upwards from beneath. They waved lazily in the air, matted together like dreadlocks.

'Stingers,' Jenine said.

Kaneesh nodded to Carla. She touched the helm to slightly change course and the boat avoided them.

'What are they?'

'Just don't touch one,' Jenine said. 'Or you'll find out.'

As she spoke, another sky-slug came into view. It was giving the creepers a wide berth, but they seemed to sense its presence and drifted towards it, as if reaching out to grasp it in a friendly embrace.

Too late, the slug took evasive action. The creepers were

upon it. They left deep, black weals where they touched its flesh. The sky-slug writhed and squirmed. Then it was suddenly quiet and the creepers enveloped it.

'Good,' Carla said. 'They won't bother with us now.'

We sailed on. I looked back. Already the creepers were unravelling. The slug had gone. There was nothing left of it. The creepers shook themselves loose and drifted down again to form a curtain. They looked decorative, attractive, even enticing; rather beautiful in their way, not lethal at all. They looked something else now too: plump, sleek, and well fed.

'Look . . .'

Jenine pointed to the side of the boat, where one of the creepers had scraped along the hull. It had left a dark trail.

'Wow . . .'

Unthinkingly, I reached out. She knocked my hand aside.

'Don't touch it. What are you doing?'

'It's still toxic?'

'Of course it is. You'll lose your fingers.'

Kaneesh brought a hose over and sprayed the hull. There was a hiss and a burst of steam and the water sizzled.

On we sailed.

Every now and then we spotted debris entangled in creepers. Or the spotlight would pick things out lying on the surface of the island below. There were the struts of masts, the remnants of sails, pieces of broken solar panels, shattered hulls, flotsam and jetsam, lost or abandoned cargoes. It was a junk dealer's paradise. Though no junk boat would venture here; they'd stick to easier and safer salvage.

'How many ships don't get through?' I asked.

'The careless ones don't,' Jenine told me.

Yet I doubted it was that simple. I didn't think it was solely a matter of skill and good skymanship. I felt you had to be lucky too.

'Why do so many risk coming this way?' I said.

'It saves days of travelling, of course. The shortcut's worth the danger. And besides, not everybody wants to use the Main Drift. There are too many custom patrols around there for some people's liking.'

I suspected that included Kaneesh. He wouldn't want to meet a customs and excise patrol. They might pull him over, ask to see his documentation, his authorisations and clearances, his licences and permissions, his identity card and all the other necessary papers that he no doubt didn't have.

They might even ask to see his tax and insurance records. Then he would definitely be in trouble. He probably hadn't paid a cent of income tax in his whole life. And he no doubt intended to keep things that way.

For the next hour we sailed steadily on, avoiding the dangling creepers and trailing fronds, and discouraging the curiosity of any passing, would-be predators, tempted to find out if we were edible. Kaneesh kept busy with the boat hook, fending off anything that got too close.

After a while he got tired – or bored – and handed the boat hook to me. So I put on a display of bravado and prodded energetically away, as I had seen him do, at any creature that ventured too near.

The spotlight on the prow cut a swathe through the darkness. Another few hours and we would be back out in the light. But just when I assumed that things would be easy and straightforward from now on, a shape loomed out of the gloom above us. It wasn't a creature this time. It was a boat. With creatures on it, certainly. But human creatures like us.

Kaneesh took the boat hook back from me.

'Carla!'

He called to draw her attention to what he and I and Jenine had just seen.

'Who are they? What is it?' I whispered.

'Barbaroons,' Jenine said. 'Proper ones. Not just water thieves. Serious pirates.'

'What do they want?'

'What do you think, Christien? What do pirates usually want? Your money, maybe?'

'I don't have any money. Well . . . not much.'

'How about your life, then? You've got one of those, haven't you? At least for the time being.'

The approaching ship was close enough for me to make out its occupants, even in that gloomy darkness. It was propelled by a galley of rowers, paddling the air with wide, flat-tipped oars. The rest of the crew lined the decks, armed with knives, cutlasses and swords. They were grim and terrifying.

And, somehow, what made them even more terrifying was that every single one of them was blind and unseeing, with sightless eyes that stared blankly, or with dark, empty hollows, like the faces of skulls.

189

But despite that, each one of them also seemed to be watching us closely, as if they could discern the very fear on our faces and the mounting dread in our hearts. I told myself not to panic, but I could feel the sweat trickling down my back.

I looked at Kaneesh and saw that even on his face small beads of perspiration were forming. If Kaneesh was worried, then there was something to worry about. And that frightened me, even more.

When even the fearless start to look fearful, you know that you've got problems.

28

barbaroons

'They've got no eyes. They can't –'

The moment the words were out of my mouth, every head on that approaching deck turned towards me.

'They don't need to . . .' Jenine whispered. The heads moved again, to face her.

Kaneesh hammered the boat hook against the side. The rattling noise lured the sightless faces to turn in his direction. He sprang along the deck, banging and crashing as he went. Then he ran across to the other side and did the same. Carla took up a knife and rapped the hilt of it against an empty basin.

'What are they doing?'

'Trying to dupe them,' Jenine said. 'To make them think there are more of us. If they imagine there's a full crew, they might not risk attacking.'

At each new sound, heads and ears turned.

'But surely everyone with any sense must try to deceive them like that?'

'That doesn't mean it won't work. They've got to decide whether to risk it; whether it's real or a bluff. Come on. Grab something. Make a noise. Loud as you can.'

We joined in the hubbub, making as much noise around the boat as we could. The Barbaroons went on listening, their heads cocked to one side; they looked like curious, exotic birds.

'How can they be pirates if they can't see?' I said, as I struck out with a ladle and whacked resoundingly at an empty water barrel.

'They live in darkness,' Jenine said. 'They don't need to see.' She rattled a cup and a bowl together.

'And if they capture a ship, what do they do?'

'Take it. And seize its cargo.'

'And the people on board?'

'Give them a choice. The way the Quenant do.'

'What choice? Choice to do what?'

'Join them or be killed.'

'But in that case –'

She already knew what I was going to say.

'In that case why are they all blind?'

'Yes,' I said.

'If you want to live, and agree to become one of them, then that's just what you become. They blind you. So you're the same as they are. No eyes. No sight. No unfair advantages. You're committed.'

'But . . . that's so – barbaric.'

'They're Barbaroons.'

'But surely, if they had someone sighted on board –'

192

'Maybe. Or maybe that someone might try to escape. Or to take over. But once you've lost your eyes, then you're with them. What other choice do you have then?'

'Plenty. The fact that you can't see doesn't mean –'

'No. But how are you to escape? Where do you escape to? Except over the side.'

'Are they going to let us by? Do you think we've fooled them?'

'Don't know – we'll soon find out.'

'Well, at least we can see.'

'Don't count on that to save you,' Jenine said. 'Don't you know about the Valley of the Blind?'

I did. It was a story we had studied once at school. There used to be a saying that, 'in the Valley of the Blind, the one-eyed man is king.' In the story, a one-eyed man hears this and so he journeys to the remote Valley of the Blind, thinking to make himself their ruler. But what he discovers is that the blind populace are far more attuned to their familiar surroundings than he will ever be. And far from becoming their king, he is forced to become their slave.

The ship drew nearer. We went on making as much racket as we could, trying to sound like a full crew: one armed to the teeth and capable of inflicting dire casualties.

But we must have tried too hard. We had overlooked the obvious: full complements of crew don't make such a commotion. A full crew would have been quieter. Even a hundred men can be silent when they have to be, holding their collective breath. A full crew might have kept deliberately quiet, to incite an attack, knowing that they would take the upper hand. They would have pretended silence. Only the outnumbered would so pathetically bang and crash in an unconvincing show of bravado.

Empty kettles make the most noise and the noise we made proved our hollowness and vulnerability. When you hear someone whistling in the dark, the chances are he's only doing it to keep his spirits up. More than likely, he's alone. He doesn't have an army, following two steps behind him.

The Barbaroons' ship was now little more than a hundred metres away. The crew lined the deck and they were certainly no beauty pageant. The ones who didn't look like killers simply looked like something worse. The kinder of them might put you out of your misery; the others would delight in putting you into it.

The one I took for the captain, if only because he was taller, broader and more vocal than the rest, was at the prow, his head held at an angle, as if his ears were eyes and he could hear what was going on as clearly as an ordinary man could see it.

He reached for a harpoon gun, raised it and aimed. Kaneesh swiftly spun the tiller, simultaneously adjusting the buoyancy of the ship. We floated up, but the other man sensed it, and he raised the harpoon gun as we ascended, following our trajectory every step of the way.

Then he pulled the trigger.

The bolt fired out and shot across the space that

separated us, embedding itself in our hull. As it did, three more harpoons simultaneously exploded and our ship was caught, like a speared fish on the end of a line.

The Barbaroons held the ropes tightly and began to winch them in. The ships drew closer. Kaneesh ran to the side and tried to hack through the securing ropes. But they were thick and took a lot of cutting and some were out of his reach. Or he would cut one rope loose, only for another bolt to embed itself into the side of the boat, coming perilously near to killing him.

He shouted to Carla. 'The pump. Start it up!'

She ran to the compressor. The Barbaroons were closing in. Their captain was cursing and yelling, laying about him indiscriminately with a lash, telling his crew to pull those ropes in, damn them, or he'd give them even worse across their backs.

Soon they'd be near enough to board us.

'The pump!' Kaneesh yelled again. 'Start that pump!'

Carla tried the compressor. It shuddered and misfired, then it caught.

The Barbaroons were so close now you could smell them. And they didn't smell good. They stank of slept-in clothes and unwashed bodies; of lice-ridden hair; of foul breath, unbrushed teeth, and rotting gums. That's one thing you don't hear so much about pirates and brigands: the fact is that for a lot of the time, they stink, to high and low heaven.

Jenine and I were with Kaneesh at the side. We were leaning over, blades in our hands, trying to hack at the harpoon ropes which tethered us. As I cut through one of them, I heard a whoosh and felt a breath of air, then heard a reverberating twang as a thrown knife embedded itself into the hull, not two centimetres from my ear.

Not a bad shot, I thought, for a blind man.

Maybe next time, he wouldn't miss.

The compressors were humming.

'Turn them up!' Kaneesh yelled. 'Top speed!'

Carla moved a lever. The hum became a loud throb, then a drone.

'All right. Now!'

Kaneesh ran to the compressor's intake hose. He grabbed its nozzle and pulled at the reel. The hose unravelled. He ran back with it to the side. There was a crash of wood on wood and metal on metal as the two boats collided. The Barbaroons were upon us now. Just a step away. Hands extended, they groped for holds; their bare, calloused feet edging their way ahead. Their knives and swords were at the ready. So close were they, I could see rust and dried blood on the blades.

'Now!' Kaneesh shouted to Carla. 'Reverse it! Full power!'

Carla threw the compressor into reverse. There was a second of silence, then a great torrent of water spumed from the hose, white and pluming, under enormous pressure. It shot out like a liquid bullet. Kaneesh had to steady himself to avoid being thrown overboard by the sheer force of the water streaming from the hose.

The jet from that water cannon hit the Barbaroons with

the force of a swung hammer. One of them, his foot already on deck, his sword held high, took the full impact of it in his chest. He was lifted bodily off his feet and swept clean over the side. All we saw of him after that was what we heard of him, as he plunged into the darkness; he landed with a muffled thud on the lower Island of Night far beneath.

More of them came to board the ship. Kaneesh repelled two of them. Carla fended one off with a boat hook. Jenine and I went on desperately trying to cut the mooring ropes. She had to lean right over, as I held onto her, in order to reach the last of them. As she hacked with her knife, the Barbaroons yelled and cursed in chaos and confusion. The water cannon knocked their legs from under them. They skidded on the deck and crashed painfully to the boards.

'That's it!'

The rope was cut. I pulled her back up.

'Full speed!' Kaneesh yelled. 'Full speed!'

He kept the water cannon trained on them while Carla went to the tiller. She opened up the engines to full power and away we sailed. We were on the reserve batteries, but it wouldn't be long until we were back in the light – if the Barbaroons didn't catch up with us first.

Behind us they came, chasing fast. The rowers had taken to the galley oars and pawed the air with those wide, flat, fan-shaped paddles. They rowed in frantic unison, with all the energy and speed they could muster.

But they couldn't outrun us. We left them trailing. They fired a last harpoon, but it fell short. Soon we could barely hear their cursing, and then I realised that I couldn't even smell them any more. Their boat was a dark, receding shape, a shadow among shadows. And so we left them to their angry disappointment and to their eternal darkness, to their brutal and violent, and probably short, lives. We left them to wait for the next unwary travellers, foolhardy enough to take a shortcut between the Islands of Night.

Kaneesh turned the compressor off. He inspected the gauges.

'Well?' Carla said.

'Empty,' he said. 'We need to find more clouds.'

But even the loss of our water seemed a small price to pay for our sight and for our lives. You only have the one life, but there is always another cloud. Well, eventually there is, if you can wait for it. And sometimes that's all you can do.

Of course, I could afford to be philosophical; it hadn't been my cargo and my livelihood. It wasn't my loss. It was theirs. It was no particular concern of mine. At least not until I got thirsty.

But it had been my life. And I was quite attached to it, and glad to have held on to it – at least for a while longer. Though for how much longer remained to be seen.

29

whaler

Soon after we emerged from that long, dark corridor between the Islands of Night, we saw some vague shapes in the middle distance, moving in our direction.

We squinted at them through eyes not yet fully reaccustomed to the light. But what we saw wasn't the bank of clouds we'd hoped for. It was something else. It was a whaler.

Jenine made it out first.

'It's a factory vessel. See the shape of the bows?'

It was a massive sky-ship, powered by two immense wind sails and myriad sun cells, which sparkled like dew. It looked more like a battleship than a trader, for on its foredeck were mounted two colossal harpoon guns, solidly bolted down.

But the surprise wasn't the boat itself – it was what was tethered to the hull. Flanking its port and starboard sides were two dead whales, each with red, vivid wounds where they had been impaled by harpoons. The whaler had killed two sky-whales so far. And now it was after a third. Another was running ahead of it, as yet oblivious to its pursuer.

'Butchers!' It was Kaneesh who spoke, quite softly and quietly too, almost without malice. Just stating an indisputable fact.

We watched with grim fascination as the whaler closed in on its quarry. The creature floated onwards, slow and gentle, innocent and oblivious, occasionally altering course with a flick of its tail – which was bigger than our boat. Its undersides were dark, its top half pale, almost pure white.

'Why do they do it? There's surely no need . . .'

The Cloud Hunters seemed to have some affinity with the creature, and a reserve of pity and sympathy for it too. Maybe whales and Cloud Hunters had something in common: born free but prone to persecution. The free are often envied, even hated, for their freedom. Some people would hunt a sky-whale or kill a sky-shark for no other reason than to say that they had done it, that they had faced one in some big game hunt, as if this were something courageous, when the things didn't have a chance. If sky-whales came equipped with their own guns and harpoons, nobody would bother them then. They wouldn't dare.

'Why do they do it?' I asked again. 'What's the point?'

'Oil, meat, fat, fuel. There are plenty of substitutes. But it's a tradition with them. The whaling islands never got civilised,' Kaneesh said.

Which I also thought was pretty good, coming from him.

'No. They just got rich and fat. They came from the dark ages and they stayed there,' Carla said.

And yet . . .

I remembered something. The perfume that Carla wore. My mother had told me that it was musk, extracted from the glands of a whale. But perhaps she had been wrong. Maybe I'd ask Jenine about it. Another time, though. Not now.

The whaling ship ignored us. We were a minnow compared to it. It sailed on in sombre majesty, steadily following the third sky-whale, which was still heedless of its pursuit

There was movement on the forecastle of the whaler. Two men went forward and took the covers off the harpoon guns; those guns looked like small missile launchers. The sailors loaded harpoons into the barrels and checked the linkage ropes, so that even if they missed, or if the whale managed to pull free, the harpoons would not be lost, but could be reeled back in for another shot.

'What can we do?' I asked Jenine. 'How can we stop them?'

'We can't,' she said. Then she seemed to think of something. 'Or maybe –' She disappeared to the wheelhouse.

She was gone no more than a minute. The marksmen on the sky-whaler were behind their guns taking aim, waiting for the command to fire.

'What's that you have?' I asked as Jenine returned.

She held a canister, the size of a small fire extinguisher. It had a red nozzle coming out of it in the shape of a horn. She had yellow foam earplugs in her ears.

'What is it?' I asked again. She hadn't heard me.

'Put your fingers in your ears,' she said.

'What?'

'I don't want to deafen you!'

I saw that Kaneesh and Carla had already done so. So, without further question, I did the same. Well, it may have muffled things, but it didn't blot them out.

First I heard the amplified command come from the sky-whaler's PA.

'Get ready, take aim . . .'

Next thing, my eardrums almost erupted.

The canister Jenine held was a compressed air siren. She set it off and it screamed out a high-decibel shriek of distress. Not content with doing it once, she did it again. And again.

At the first burst of noise the sky-whale slowed and looked curiously around. At the second, it panicked. The third time, it simply put its head down, expelled all the air in its lungs to lose buoyancy, and dived.

To be more accurate, it plummeted. Within seconds it was a fish-sized figure far below us. Then we saw it level off and resume its placid grazing.

A torrent of amplified abuse came at us from the sky-whaler. But, as Jenine said, what could they do? She hadn't done anything criminal. Just tested out our emergency siren. And fortunately, it was in good working order.

All the same, to be on the safe side, Kaneesh uncovered the solar panels and in seconds we were streaking away from the whaler and were soon out of range of its harpoons – just in case they had any ideas.

'They already had two sky-whales,' Jenine said. 'That was bad enough. How many can someone eat?'

She went to put the canister back in the wheelhouse.

Her mother had taken the helm and Kaneesh was at his usual place on deck, staring out at the blank, blue sky, with that inscrutable, impenetrable expression on his face. You could have hung a sign on him, saying, *Do Not Disturb.* He was at his favourite pastime: looking for clouds. And he never once seemed to get bored with it.

It took us a full day to find fresh clouds and compress them into water. By then we were half a day's journey off course. Kaneesh had 'smelled' water after a few hours, but it had taken time to find it, and for the 'smell' to turn into substance.

Whether he really had 'smelled' water, or whether he had just taken a guess and got lucky, I didn't know. I certainly wasn't going to ask him or cast doubt on his abilities.

The cloud bank we found was dense and cold. As soon as we entered it, Jenine and I turned on the compressors and slowly the tanks refilled. There was nothing to do then except to wait. I joined Jenine at the stern of the ship.

'So what do we do?' I said.

'What do we do when?'

'Well, now?' I said. 'Once the tanks are full.'

'We go and sell the water,' she said. 'To the Dissenters.'

'And then?'

'Then we go to the Forbidden Isles and find my father. And free him.'

'And how exactly do we do that?' I said. 'Rescue your father? Have you considered that might not be so easy?'

'We don't expect it to be easy. We don't expect anything to be easy.'

She walked off to check on the tank pressure. I followed her.

'Jenine, you're not facing up to it. I mean, how, precisely, do we dock on the Forbidden Isle of Quenant,' I persisted. 'Without being seen? And go on land without being noticed? Then walk around, complete strangers and foreigners, and no one remarking on it? Then track down your father, simply let him out of jail, and get away without anybody doing anything about it? Do you even know where he's held?'

She gave me one of her cold, indifferent stares, as if to tell me again that I was an outsider and always would be and was only there under sufferance.

'Don't worry,' she said. 'You won't have to do anything dangerous. We're not expecting that. Just wait in the boat and make sure no one boards it, and have it ready for our escape when we return.'

'And how do I do that? On an island full of religious crackpots? Who have nooses dangling from every crack and crevice? And whose means of dealing with people they don't like is to hang them?'

'You only have to dock to let us onto the land. Then you can hover offshore.'

'What if they see me?'

'What if they do?'

'Won't they come after me?'

'Why should they? You won't have done anything. If they do bother you, you can drift off into international air space. You have to set foot on their land before they'll actually do anything.'

'Won't they chase after us when you come back with your father?' (I really meant 'if you ever come back', but didn't feel it would help to say so.)

'They might do, yes. They probably will.'

'So what then?'

'We outrun them.'

'And if we don't?'

'We fight them.'

'And if we lose? We get hanged, I suppose.'

Jenine smiled. Her scars always helped to make her smiles sardonic.

'You know, Christien,' she said. 'You're always looking for what might go wrong. You worry too much.'

'Best to be prepared,' I said.

'Oh – boy scout!' she said.

'Hope for the best, expect the worst, take what comes,' I said, quoting one of my father's dictums. 'Seems like a pretty sensible way of looking at things to me.'

'OK. So we'll take what comes, then.' She tapped the water gauge. 'Tanks are full,' she said. 'We can turn the compressors off.'

She was right. They were full to the brim. Water was spilling out of the overflow valves. The ship felt heavier again, more stable, full of ballast.

'Right,' she said. 'We can sail now. The Isles of Dissent it is. Or do you want dropping off?'

'No. The Isles of Dissent it is, I guess,' I said. 'After all, you only live once.'

'You're right about that,' she said.

So we agreed on something.

Kaneesh and Carla were already busy with the solar panels.

'And I'll tell you what else,' Jenine said. 'I'm starving. Once we're underway, I'm going to cook some dinner.'

Kaneesh powered up the reserve engines to take us out of the cloud.

'What are you thinking of cooking?' I called to Jenine.

'What do you think?' she said. 'I'll give you two guesses.'

And right enough, it was what I thought.

30

witness

I had heard plenty about the weird ways of the inhabitants of the Isles of Dissent. And like most people who have heard plenty and seen nothing for themselves, I was no doubt filled with much groundless prejudice.

Dissenters had a reputation for doing as little as they could and for taking as long as possible to do it. They were, in short, generally believed to be a bunch of long-haired, layabout anarchists who only believed in having a good time. They disliked all authority and took it as a truism that the majority is always wrong and the minority is always discriminated against.

But as we neared the Isles of Dissent, instead of the expected chaos and dilapidation, I saw only rows of tidy and well-looked-after houses and there was every sign of activity. Nets were neatly stacked and folded on the dock-side. Sky-trawlers were being painted and their decks scrubbed clean. It looked like any other island: busy, orderly and alive with activity.

It occurred to me then that really there is very little difference in the way that people live, at least compared to the vast gulfs of difference between what people believe in. But what did all these differences of belief amount to in the end? A few habits and rituals? A few dietary restrictions? And if that was really all it was, why did people bother to fight about it? Yet they did. Constantly and unremittingly. People will kill each other over nothing more than a difference of opinion – and feel every justification for doing it. It seems the hardest thing in the world is to put up with beliefs, views and opinions that don't coincide with your own.

'Ahoy! Cloud Hunters!'

The sky ahead was empty. Then I turned around, surprised to see another boat, gaining up on us.

Sky-boats can move as silently as the dust when on solar power alone. Even a shoal of sky-fish makes more disturbance. This ship had crept up on us, unheard and unseen. Had it been manned by a pack of Barbaroons, we'd already have had our throats cut.

Fortunately the ship carried friendlier faces. And one look at those faces told me all I needed to know: they were Cloud Hunters too: tall and dark, muscular and slender. There were tattoos on their bodies, and the usual assortment of amulets and bracelets around their necks, wrists and arms.

'Kaneesh!'

The man who greeted him looked nearly as disreputable

as he did: white teeth, knife, tattoos, scars, and notches carved into the boat mast.

'Eldar! How goes it?'

There were five people on board: a man, a woman, a baby, a young girl, and an older boy, about my age. I didn't like the look of him much, and I don't think he liked the look of me. I didn't altogether care for the way he was smiling at Jenine. Not that she seemed particularly interested. But having no real grounds for jealousy never stopped anyone. If anything, the flimsier the grounds, the greener the monster.

There was something different about him. I soon realised what. Unlike Jenine and the adults, his face was unmarked. But it wasn't to stay that way much longer. And that, we discovered, was the reason the boat had been speeding to catch us.

Cloud Hunters don't ordinarily waste time socialising when they have work to do. It's a different matter during the slack season or when idling in port. Then they might take things easy, and get together to swap stories and news.

But sometimes, even when work is at its busiest, custom and ritual demand attention. Work or no work, tradition must take brief precedence.

The fenders of the other boat clattered against ours as it pulled over. The boats were secured, then there was a brief discussion over who should join whom; it being the more coveted role to play the host rather than the guest.

However, when Eldar announced that he had pulled alongside because there was to be a 'Witnessing' (and I give it a capital letter because that was how he spoke of it – in capital letters and portentous tones) then Carla and Kaneesh agreed that we should go on board their vessel, which we did.

The newcomers greeted me with a polite but cool reserve. Jenine explained who I was and how they had let me come along on this voyage. Eldar and his wife brewed up green tea and poured it into small bowls which they offered round. I tasted it, but it was disgusting, and I looked for an opportunity to pour it over the side.

They all made conversation for a while, discussing the weather, trade, the price of water and where the best clouds were to be found these days. They talked of people they knew, of births and marriages, illnesses and deaths. But there was no mention of the Forbidden Islanders, nor Jenine's father's imprisonment, nor talk of revenge killings. That was private, family business.

Finally they got around to the matter in hand.

'So your son is growing up now?' Kaneesh said.

'Of age from three days ago,' Eldar told him. 'You're the first hunters we've seen, able to witness – if you will.'

'Of course,' Kaneesh nodded. 'Our honour.'

I didn't yet know what was going on, but it didn't take much to surmise. And my assumptions soon grew to certainties when I saw the increasingly apprehensive look on the face of Eldar's son. He looked like someone about to have a tooth extracted and who was trying to give the impression that he was quite indifferent to the prospect. Only he was not entirely succeeding.

The son's name was Alain. Jenine was talking to him. They stood together by the wheel. She appeared to be explaining something to him and her hand indicated her face. Her fingers traced out her scars.

His mother took a bowl of the green tea over to him. I noticed that before she did so, she broke open a phial containing a clear, colourless liquid, which she poured into the cup – some kind of anaesthetic or painkiller, I presumed, to numb his nerve endings for a while.

There was a little more conversation, but it seemed to be for a calculated duration, as if to give the drug time to take effect. Then the talking was over. Eldar went to the centre of the boat and announced, somewhat theatrically:

'Friends: the Witnessing . . .'

He paused, as if for dramatic effect, like an actor on a stage.

'They'll think it's a great honour for you to see this,' Jenine whispered to me. But I wasn't altogether sure that 'honour' was the word I would have chosen.

'Alain . . .'

Eldar beckoned to his son, who joined his father at the mast.

On a brazier on deck lay an ornamental knife with an inlaid handle, its blade resting on the hot embers.

'Friends . . .' Eldar said again. 'Our son begins the journey to manhood today. Just as your daughter here – ' he addressed his remarks to Carla ' – began her journey to become a young woman.'

There was some serious nodding in affirmation of this.

211

'Today,' Eldar continued, 'is a time to put away the trivial things of childhood and to enter fully into whatever destiny may lie ahead. To join the community and fellowship of hunters – as witnessed here by our friends and neighbours, who honour us with their presence. And in the presence of this invited stranger.' (That was me.)

There was more nodding and murmuring from Carla and Kaneesh, who politely denied that they were honouring anyone, but that the honour was all theirs in being asked to attend upon such a momentous and significant event.

Then Alain leaned back against the mast and turned his face up towards the sky.

His father reached to the brazier and took up the knife; its sharp, stiletto blade glowed red.

Alain's little sister started to cry. Her mother picked her up and held her. The baby was snuffling, asleep in its cradle.

Alain closed his eyes. His father plunged the dagger into a bowl of water. There was a whoosh and a sizzle of steam.

'Be brave, Alain,' I heard his mother say. And she looked at Eldar as if to say, 'And you be careful and don't make any mistakes.'

Then he did it.

He took the knife and brought it up to his son's face.

'Don't move,' he said quietly. 'Steady now . . .'

He aimed the tip of the blade at a point high on his son's left cheekbone, so close to the eye that the incision all but cut through the lower lashes.

Alain winced, but didn't cry out. His jaw clenched visibly.

His father slowly and precisely moved the knife down along towards his son's mouth. A streak of red followed the path of the blade as it cut into his face, almost as if the knife were a fine brush, painting a line. But the line rapidly turned ragged, as the spots of red widened into blotches and then into drops which ran and trickled down his face.

But still he said nothing, not a murmur. His eyes remained shut and his jaw clenched as his father cleaned the tip of the knife by swirling it around in the bowl of water. Then he brought the point up to just under his son's right eye, and repeated the whole process, carving a second deep and ugly incision into what – even I had to admit – was a fairly handsome face.

How can you do that? I thought. How can you? To your own son?

But I understood that for Eldar, the greater crime would have been not to do it, not to initiate his son into this ceremony of manhood. To have left him without scars would have been to ostracise him from his own family, to turn him into an outcast, without identity or tribe.

Yet all the same it seemed very cruel and brutal to mark your children's faces, and to subject them to that sharp, unforgiving knife.

Blood was all over him now. It was as if he were crying blood, as if it were pouring from his eyes in great red tears. It dripped from his face onto his bare torso and ran to the waistband of his clothes.

'It's done,' Eldar said. 'And done well.'

Alain opened his eyes. He actually smiled.

His mother brought a cloth to wipe away and staunch the blood, and she held up a bowl which seemed to contain a paste of herbs and aromatics.

Pleased and proud, Eldar embraced his son. Kaneesh and Carla and Jenine applauded the moment, and I naturally joined in with the general congratulations, if only out of politeness, though in all honesty, I felt a bit sick.

Carla disappeared for a moment, back to our boat; when she returned she brought a bracelet, in the shape of a coiled snake, which she presented to Eldar's son. He thanked her and put it around his wrist.

His own mother, meanwhile, was concocting some kind of poultice. She made Alain sit down on deck, with his head tilted back, and applied the mixture to the two wounds.

'Won't the scars just close up?' I asked Jenine.

'The mixture will get inside them,' she said. 'It makes them heal faster and it also turns them black.'

I looked at her facial scars. I had always assumed that they had been done when she had been much younger. But they must have been far more recent than I had supposed. Had they been done when she was an infant, they might have closed up, becoming almost invisible as she had grown.

She saw me staring.

'You next?' she said. 'If you want be a Cloud Hunter?'

But before I could think of an answer, she had gone over to talk to Alain.

214

I felt vaguely envious. I didn't know why. I didn't want my face sliced open. But I couldn't help but think that if I did have a couple of scars like theirs I'd look pretty mean and cool, or at least a bit interesting. My mother would have had a heart attack of course. But you can't please everybody.

Alain sat recovering, smiling forbearingly, being congratulated on his new status and praised for his stoicism in achieving it. A second round of green tea was brewed and drunk (or discreetly poured over the side) with the same ceremony as before.

But once this was finished, it was plain that the ritual was over and that Eldar and his family were as anxious and impatient to be on their way as we were to be on ours.

The thing had been done; the matter had been witnessed; there would be plenty of time for more elaborate celebrations. But for now there were clouds to harvest and water to sell. Hunters hunted and trackers tracked; it wasn't in their nature to stand around and make small talk for the sake of it. Cloud Hunters were nomads and wanderers; their inner spirit told them to keep moving and never really to stop for longer than was necessary. It was the travelling, the journey itself, that mattered to them. I don't think they cared all that much for the destination. That could have been anywhere.

'Well, my friends . . .'

Kaneesh began on the brief formalities which preceded the farewells. They shook hands, embraced each other, vowed to meet again soon, then wished each other good hunting and good luck.

There were some private words, probably of congratulation, for Alain from Carla and Kaneesh, and small presents for the baby and the little girl, who one day would both have scars on their pretty, angelic faces too.

Eldar shook my hand and thanked me for my Witnessing, saying that for an outsider to stand witness to a coming of age was propitious and a good omen.

Whether that was so, or whether he was just saying it to be polite, or because he liked the sound of it, I didn't know. But it had a ring of sincerity about it.

So I responded in kind and told him what a great and rare honour it was for me to be present – which, I suppose, it was – and that I was lucky to be among the fortunate few who had been allowed to stand witness to the coming of age of a Cloud Hunter.

I appeared to have hit the right note in saying this. Even Kaneesh nodded approvingly, as if to confirm that I had said something apt and sensible at last, and was showing some faint promise of not turning out to be a complete idiot after all. I had opened my mouth, and to my credit, something that made sense had come out.

Alain came over and shook my hand. The cuts in his face had stopped bleeding, but he looked very odd and sinister, with the now drying lines of mashed herbs tapering down towards his mouth.

I didn't feel so badly disposed towards him now that they were leaving. Jenine had been a mite too interested

216

in him for my liking though. It was all right for him with his scars. He had all the advantages, not like me. I had to make my own way in the world.

I knew that Jenine might move on one day. And that I might never see her again. I knew it and so did she.

People say that you don't know what you've got till it's gone. But it's not always so. Sometimes you do know what you have, and just what you stand to lose, and how hard it will be to lose it when the time comes.

Later that day, as we sat on deck after the meal, Jenine turned to me. 'You were jealous back then, weren't you, Christien?' she said. 'I saw it in your eyes.'

'No, I wasn't,' I said. Then added, 'Jealous of what?'

'His scars.'

'Maybe –'

'I'm glad you don't have them,' she said.

'You are?'

'Yes. Your face is fine as it is.'

'No room for improvement?'

She laughed. 'I didn't say that. There's always room for improvement.'

'I'll work on it then,' I said.

'Yes,' she said. 'You do that.'

And she seemed to think herself highly amusing. But I didn't see what was so funny.

'Oh, Christien –' she said.

'What?' I said.

'Nothing,' she said. 'Nothing. You don't need to change. You're all right just as you are.'

'Ditto,' I said. 'You too.'

'Thanks for the compliment,' she said. Then: 'That's quite some charm offensive you've got there, isn't it?'

But sometimes you don't really know what to say, do you? Or you know what you want to say, but it doesn't come out as you intended.

Life's a complicated business.

31

dissenters

The Isles of Dissent radiated out from a large, central island, like moons around a planet. The main settlement, the town of Dissent, to which we were headed, contained most of the Dissenters. Here were the minorities and the individualists, all the square pegs who had found only round holes elsewhere. Here were left-handed people, who had fled from the Right Only Isle. Living alongside them were right-handed neighbours, who had abandoned the Left Alone Isle for similar, if diametrically opposite, reasons.

Why had the left-handed not gone instead to the Left Alone Isle, where they would have been welcomed? And vice versa? The reason was that they wanted to live where difference was tolerated, not in a place where conformity was the law.

As we came in to dock, I sensed apprehension on the quayside. Men and women stopped working. They shielded their eyes and watched us approach. One man disappeared into a building and returned carrying a crossbow; others appeared with cudgels and clubs. Tolerant the Dissenters may have been, but that didn't mean they weren't prepared to defend themselves.

But once the boat was recognised, and they heard Kaneesh shouting his greetings, they put the weapons away and stood by with mooring ropes so we could tie up to the jetty.

Once close enough to see their faces, I realised that their skin was dry and their lips were cracked. Notices on the harbour wall warned: WATER IS YOUR LIFE BLOOD – DO NOT WASTE IT.

So they were more than glad to see us. Even with their own compressors running flat out, they could never extract enough water from the atmosphere to be self-sufficient. The Isles of Dissent just happened to be in a place where cloud rarely formed and rain seldom fell.

Their vapour compressors were old, too, and always breaking down. The Forbidden Islanders, a short journey away, had storehouses of spare parts. But they wouldn't trade, not with Dissenters.

The only 'heathens' the Forbidden Islanders would trade with were Cloud Hunters, and that only because they wanted their water and because they would soon be moving on – not moving in next door. It is always easier to get on with people who you know aren't going to stay.

Which made me think again about Jenine's father. There was still something I needed to say to her.

So, when we disembarked, glad to feel solid ground under

our feet again – though it was hard to lose that sensation of being on a boat – I asked her to take a walk with me and to show me the island. We left Kaneesh and Carla to deal with the Dissenters and to pump the water out from the boat and into the waiting transporters on the quay.

We followed a rocky path from the harbour, leading up to the hills above the town of Dissent. We could view the whole island from here: see the harbour and the ships and the gleaming glass of the greenhouses on the hills, where the Dissenters grew their food.

'Jenine,' I said, 'I've been thinking.'

'Again? What about this time?'

'Well, a lot of things, really. But about your father – and the Forbidden Isles.'

'I've been thinking about that too,' she said. 'I owe you an apology. It wasn't fair to deceive you as to where we were going.'

'No,' I said. 'It's all right. I'll go with you. I want to.'

'Then what?'

'I just wondered, when we get there, if it's right that I should merely stay with the boat.'

She looked at me quizzically.

'Well, if you come on shore with us, you might get hanged. I don't think your parents would be too pleased.'

'No, but look, the thing is – the three of you, it's obvious who you are. The moment you set foot on land, if the Quenant see your faces, they'll know.'

'They won't see our faces. We'll cover up.'

'Yes, but me, I've got no scars. No one's going to

221

challenge me. Not as readily. So maybe I should come with you. I won't have to be hooded. It'll look all the more natural and less suspicious if at least one of us doesn't have his head covered and his face hidden.'

She looked thoughtful.

'And why would you do that for us?'

'I just would. To help you. As friends.'

'We're Cloud Hunters, Christien,' she said. 'The only real friends we've ever had were people like ourselves.'

She started back down the stony track.

'But I am like you,' I called after her. 'We're all like each other, aren't we?'

She stopped and turned.

'No,' she said. 'Not really. Your world's entirely different. You can be anything. You have choices – infinite possibilities. What do I have? A destiny. No choice at all. Can't you see that?'

'Then why did you let me come along with you, if you didn't like me? If we're not friends?'

She sighed. But she waited for me.

'Christien, I never said I didn't like you,' she said. 'Maybe I like you a bit too much. Maybe that's what makes it so difficult.'

But she didn't walk on until I had caught up with her, and then we returned to the boat together.

Maybe she was right that Cloud Hunters didn't have many friends. But then neither did I. So at least we had something in common. But the friends I did have, I valued greatly.

*   *   *

When we got back to the boat, the last drops of water were trickling into the storage tanks on the dockside. Carla and Kaneesh were involved in deep negotiations with a group of Dissenters. They were haggling in Common Dialect – which, despite its alleged ubiquity throughout the islands as an international business tongue, nobody ever seemed to speak very well.

I understood enough to know that they were predictably arguing to get the best price for their water. Whatever had been agreed before unloading – and surely something had – was being renegotiated now that the water had been discharged. Kaneesh was threatening to pump all the water back on board. Cloud Hunters and Dissenters have nothing against a good, long, satisfactory haggle when they do business.

They finally agreed on a figure, shook hands on it, and the money was paid. Some crates of greenhouse-grown fruits and vegetables were then loaded on board, and we were free to sail.

But the Cloud Hunters didn't seem in any immediate hurry to leave. So we left the boat unattended – there was no fear of anything being stolen – and walked with some of the Dissenters into town. There we found a cafe and sat down to eat a proper dinner at a decent table – a table that wasn't moving up and down, and a meal that wasn't sky-fish. I realised how accustomed I had become to the perpetual motion of a sky-ship, which is always bobbing on the thermals of the air like a cork on water.

After the meal we strolled around, then made our way

back. Kaneesh stopped on the way and went into a shop, to re-emerge with a small bundle and a satisfied smile.

He unwrapped the bundle when we got to the boat. He had bought himself a new knife. And it wasn't the kind you cut your bread with, more the sort you'd use for slitting throats and severing ligaments. He tried out its throwing potential and nodded with approval as it embedded itself with a pleasant twang into the mast.

We rested a while then, lying on deck under a canopy strung up to keep out the sun. I must have slept for over an hour. When I opened my eyes, I was beneath a blanket which someone had thrown over me. The air was cooler and preparations were being made to get underway.

The quayside was now deserted. The island was asleep. We slipped the ropes free from the capstans and stole quietly away into the equally silent and empty sky.

The time passed. We entered a bank of cloud. I thought we might stop to turn the compressors on and to fill the tanks, but no, we just gathered up what we could as we kept sailing. I guessed they wanted to keep the boat as light as possible, to be able to get away in any pursuit.

The dots in the sky ahead of us grew larger, turning from dots to blots to islands. With binoculars you could see their shapes and make out which islands they were from the sky-charts. Here we finally were, at the Forbidden Isles.

As we drew near, name signs became visible at the harbours. First we passed the Isle of the Chosen. Then, the Isle of the Blessed; the Isle of the Master; the Isle of the Wanted; the Isle of the Select; the Isle of the Righteous; the Isle of the Covered Heads. And so on and on.

Next to those signs proclaiming an island's affiliation and allegiance, were other signs, announcing in no uncertain terms who was not to set foot there, except at peril of their lives.

No Whites, I saw, as our boat drifted by one island. Then, No Blacks at another. No Browns at a third. Then, No Lefts, No Rights, No Drinkers, No Abstainers, No Bare Heads, No Hats and, believe it or not, No Dogs. And at one, I saw: No Cloud Hunters.

The very rocks of the islands seemed to glare at you with hostility and suspicion as you sailed past, as if the crags had eyes and were on the lookout for anyone with the wrong kind of customs or the wrong beliefs – as if all this could be discerned by the simple act of staring; as if rocks could see into your soul.

We sailed on. Kaneesh was at the prow. He turned his glance, with magnificent disdain and an expression of consummate disgust, upon every island we passed, as if they were all several fathoms beneath his contempt, but he was favouring them with it anyway.

I felt a sense of not belonging to, and of being shunned by, each isle we passed. Many had guns and cannon mounted on battlements at their harbours, as if afraid that some wind of change might blow to ruffle their flags and their certainties, and they had to be prepared to protect themselves from it.

The air around those islands all but crackled with malice

and intolerance, as if everyone in the vicinity were spoiling for a fight, just waiting for some defiant stranger to come along and deny the prevailing belief. So that those who knew better could make a convert of him, or – more enjoyably – a martyr.

It was not enough for these people to be right, or to believe themselves so. What was far more important was that others had to be proved wrong. Others had to be enlightened, to be shown the errors of their ways and the falsity of their opinions. Nothing more delighted the heart of the true believers than the sight of an outnumbered heretic, fallen helplessly into their clutches.

At the hub of this archipelago of Forbidden Isles was the largest in the sector, the Isle of Quenant, to which we were headed. And here it now was, looming into our sights.

'That's it,' Jenine said. 'Have a look.'

She handed me the binoculars. I saw the place clearly and unmistakably. On its highest hill, dominating the whole island, was the outline of a massive gibbet, and suspended from that, in dark silhouette, was a great noose. You could have hanged a sky-whale from it.

32

sign of the noose

'The lovely Isle of Quenant,' Jenine said. 'That's it, and that's them. That's where my father is. Locked in some dungeon.'

I moved the binoculars and focused on the docks. Another gibbet stood at the harbour's edge, its noose dangling like a warning to you to keep sailing. 'Don't even think of parking here!' it seemed to say.

'We're not landing at the harbour, I take it?'

'Oh no,' she said. 'They'd take us prisoner in a minute.'

Kaneesh altered course; we angled away from the island; then he changed tack again. Still keeping a safe and considerable distance from the shore, we circled around it. A rugged, unpopulated coastline presented itself to our view, with innumerable coves and inlets: a smuggler's paradise – had any smugglers thought the place worth the risk.

Carla reduced the sails and we floated with the thermals. 'What now?' I said.

'We wait till the sleeping time. Then, when they're quiet, we'll go in.'

So we waited and we drifted. If we drifted too far out, Carla briefly powered the engines to bring us back in towards land. The time drifted, too, going slowly by at its own leisurely pace.

I wished there was something we could do to make it move faster. But time wasn't to be hurried that day. It shuffled along, like an old man with a walking stick, moving with interminably slow steps.

Finally, the hour arrived. We glided into a deserted cove at an unpopulated part of the island. It took some manoeuvring to get the boat in and to thread it past needle rocks and ragged outcrops. But at last we tied up at a sheltered, well-hidden spot.

'So what now? I wait here? Or what do I do?' I asked.

Jenine shook her head.

'I told my mother and Kaneesh what you said. I told them about your offer. They want you to come with us – if that's what you still want to do.'

'Of course,' I said. 'What about the boat?'

'No one will find it here. And no one's going to steal it even if they did,' she said. 'No one dare steal anything here.'

'Why not?'

'Why do you think? There's only the one penalty here for all crimes. Serious or trivial, the punishment's the same. A piece of rope's the cure for all ailments.'

I didn't really believe that the Quenant were ever going

to hang me. Not even if they did catch us. Not me. Kaneesh, Jenine and Carla, maybe. But I was from a respectable, well-off family. When I told them who my parents were, surely they'd let me go. It just goes to show how naive and stupid I was. But it didn't take me long to learn better.

'So let's go then,' I said, 'if we're going. Before I change my mind.'

'All right. Let's get it done.'

We left the boat behind us in that hidden cove and scrambled up the rocks. From the clifftop the boat was unnoticeable, unless you went to the very edge of the escarpment and peered down.

On the land side, three or four kilometres down from us, in a hill-sheltered valley, Quenant City stood in all its dubious glory. It looked like something from the Dark Ages. And the closer we got to it, the darker and more pestiferous it seemed, with endless alleyways and numerous narrow streets, criss-crossing each other and running in all directions. A map of the place would have looked like a plate of tangled spaghetti.

It was the sleeping time still. There was no natural night on this island, so the inhabitants created their own, with canopies and shades, with blinds and drapes, with heavy blackout curtains and shutters to block out the light.

We walked on, soft-footed and unspeaking, past the first crop of outlying houses. On the upper floors the blinds were pulled and the curtains drawn. But downstairs you could see into the empty rooms. In the lower windows of each house there dangled a small noose. It was a sign of

229

belief and belonging, no doubt, a certificate of allegiance. The only thing you might have hung in such a small noose was a puppet. But even so, they still gave you the creeps.

By the time we entered the city itself, there was the smell of baking bread in the air. Other than the bakers, nobody seemed awake yet. Kaneesh, Jenine and Carla pulled the hoods of their capes up to keep their faces in shadow and to hide their scars.

'Do you know where we're going?' I asked Jenine.

'Kaneesh does. He knows others who have been here. They told him the way to the centre and to the dungeons.'

So he went ahead and led us on. We walked deeper and deeper into that warren of streets that was becoming the city of Quenant.

It could have been any island capital really, if not for those nooses. They were suspended in every window and hanging from every door, like so many good luck (or was it bad luck?) charms.

We had passed a few roadside shrines on our way too, and in each there had been a noose. In some there was also a small gibbet, with a little figurine of a hanging man, his hands bound and his eyes blindfolded. In mock, carved parchment with ornamental flourishings had been written, *Quenant the Martyr*. And, *Beloved Quenant Be Our Guide*.

'But what do they actually *believe* in?' I whispered to Jenine, as we walked on. 'Other than hanging people?'

She shrugged.

'They believe they're right, of course,' she said.

'But about what?'

'Everything. About their interpretation of who God is and what happens to people when they die. About the correct and only form of worship. About how the world was created. All the usual things.'

'And that's it?'

'That's always it, isn't it?' she said, giving me a sharp look, as if I were being foolish. 'When's it any different? When's it ever anything else?' she added.

And she put on a turn of speed in order to keep up with Kaneesh and Carla, who were hurrying along ahead.

We had good reason to hurry. We hadn't timed things as well as we had intended. The sleeping time was nearly over. The Quenant were early risers.

The city was waking and coming to life. People stumbled out of doorways. Traffic moved on the streets. There were trundling handcarts and rattling barrows. Everything was done by man and woman power. There appeared to be no powered vehicles. No pack animals either. Maybe they'd all been hanged.

The most startling thing was that every person we saw wore a small noose around their neck; they sported them like neckties or cravats. Even children wore the same thing: smaller and more brightly coloured maybe, fashioned from cotton rather than string or reed, but a noose just the same.

Kaneesh ducked into a narrow, deserted back alley and beckoned us to follow. He stopped and looked around.

Spotting a length of twine which someone had coiled around a post, he took his knife, cut the twine to unravel it, then cut it again into four equal pieces. He handed us one each, took his own piece, fashioned it into a small noose, and slipped it over his head.

We copied his example. Though I don't pretend that my noose was as good as it could have been. But then I didn't have much experience of tying them.

More suitably attired to blend in with the locals, and feeling a mite less conspicuous, we ventured back out into the wider thoroughfare. In the few minutes it had taken us to fashion the nooses, it seemed that half the doors of the city had simultaneously opened and half of its inhabitants had tumbled out.

The streets were truly alive now, busy with yawning and bleary people going about their morning business and starting the day. Stalls and shops were opening; shutters were rolled back; doors were unlocked; produce was put on display. And everyone we saw – without exception – wore a noose.

A woman approached us, expensively dressed. There was a noose around her neck too. But this one was fashioned from precious stones that flashed and sparkled. She nodded graciously to a well-attired gentleman coming the other way.

'Good morning, Believer.'

'Good morning to you, Believer,' he responded. And he made a gesture with his hand, as if tracing the shape of a noose in the air, and she responded with the same movement, and they went their separate ways.

'The Sign of the Noose,' Jenine whispered.

But I had already deduced what it was. In fact, I could feel my fingers attempting the gesture for themselves, as if in fascinated, compulsive imitation.

We came to a busy square. On the corner, judging from its dome and spire, was a place of worship.

Kaneesh stopped and hesitated. I'd so far thought of him as a man devoid of curiosity outside of his own affairs, but even he seemed to want to look inside.

We went to the door of the church and slipped in. At its far end was an altar, and hanging above the altar, suspended from a beam was a noose, woven in intricate fashion from gold and silver threads. A light burned in a red glass holder.

A priest was leading a small congregation in prayer. He too wore a noose around his neck, but an elaborately woven, ceremonial one – unlike the poorer, mere twine and cotton ones of the faithful. A second noose was around his waist, worn as a belt on his cassock.

The congregation held hymn books, and many had nooses in their hands. I saw that these nooses were knotted and that the knots made the nooses seem like rosaries, while the knots themselves were the beads.

'Brethren, now we will briefly say our Stations of the Noose.'

The priest took the lead; the congregation responded. The dangling noose above the altar moved in a draught coming from an open window. The noose seemed to nod, as if giving advice and good counsel, proffering a word to the wise, warning you to be good. Or else.

I felt a tap on my shoulder. It was Jenine. Kaneesh and Carla had already gone. I followed her to the door we had come in by, and we slipped back out into the street.

The city was growing ever busier by the minute, and the closer we came to its centre, the more evident it was that preparations for some great festival were underway. There were signs and advertisements and sale boards every-where.

Quenant the Martyr. Buy Your New Noose for Quenant's Day.

Quenant's Day Cards: On Sale Here.

Grand Hanging Souvenir Programme. When Kaneesh saw that, he stopped and gave me some money,

'Go in, boy,' he said, pointing to one of the souvenir programmes on display in a shop window. 'Buy one.'

I did. When I came out with the purchase he snatched it from me, without bothering about his change. Carla and Jenine looked over his shoulder as he flicked through it.

'Ah. Here . . .'

I looked too. He was pointing at a page headed: *Quenant's Day Events.* The relevant part read: *Ceremonial Execution of Prisoners.*

'Noon,' Carla whispered. 'Noon tomorrow.'

'Tomorrow,' Kaneesh said. And he folded up the programme and twisted it in his hands as if he wanted to wring its neck.

Fortunately, Kaneesh and Carla and Jenine were not the only ones in capes and hoods that morning. There were plenty of others too. It seemed to be the local fashion to cover your head when out in the street.

So, more absorbed by the crowd than standing out from it, we followed what was now turning into a throng and moved deeper into the city.

33

beggar

There was ever more evidence that tomorrow was a special day; there were souvenirs on offer everywhere. Miniature Quenant's Day gallows were lined up for sale on the traders' stalls. There were Quenant's Day nooses and Quenant's Day key rings, Quenant's Day badges and Quenant's Day hats, Quenant's Day pens and Quenant's Day pencil sharpeners, and even – in case of rain – Quenant's Day umbrellas.

In the windows of the bakeries were loaves of Quenant's Day bread, along with Quenant's Day cakes and buns, alongside pastries that might have been croissants or bagels, but which, on closer inspection, proved to be edible nooses, made of gingerbread and glistening with sugar.

Each shop, without exception, had a small religious display in its window, of noose and gallows and hanging man, testifying to the proprietor's diligent observance of, and fidelity to, the faith.

All in all, it was quite like Christmas must once have

been (if what I had read about it was to be believed) with a festive and celebratory feeling in the air. Something unusual and exciting was on the way; something to look forward to.

It was hard to believe, from the atmosphere, that the high spot of tomorrow's celebrations was to be the Ceremonial Execution of Prisoners. But it was. It was the great highlight of the day. And among those prisoners would be Jenine's father.

'Look at them,' Jenine whispered to me. 'They're as good as mad. All going about with nooses around their necks. Yet they act as if it's perfectly normal.'

'But it is normal,' I said. 'For here. And anyway . . .' A thought struck me. 'What do Cloud Hunters believe in?'

'In keeping moving and staying out of trouble,' she said. 'There's never been a better philosophy.'

'It was keeping moving that got you into this trouble,' I pointed out.

'Well, staying put doesn't exactly seem to keep some people out of trouble either, does it, Christien?' she said. 'After all, there you were, safely sitting at home, but was it enough for you –?' And she gave me her irresistible smile.

I guess there was some truth in what she said.

We had arrived at the main square. To our left was a cathedral. I looked up to see its rising spire taper to a gibbet, from which the usual and expected noose was suspended. The cathedral doors were open and the chant of plainsong came from within.

Beggars were gathered on the cathedral steps, soliciting alms, their voices ringing out over the precinct. They sat like living, or near-dead, bundles of rags, their faces half hidden in cowls and hoods, as if to add to their appearance of dejection and misery, and to more effectively touch the onlooker's heart.

'A little charity, Believers! For Quenant's sake! Alms for a poor man! Alms! Have no qualms, give alms!'

Kaneesh flipped one of the beggars a coin. It landed by the man's feet and he seized upon it as if it were food for the starving. He snatched it up and hid it within his robes before anyone else could get it.

In the square, workmen were busy, banging and clattering with hammers and nails, building a podium and constructing gibbets upon it, from which tomorrow's executions would no doubt be carried out.

'Where is your father being held?' I whispered. 'Where is the prison?'

'There is no real prison in Quenant,' Jenine said.

'No prison?'

'Just a few cells here, under the town hall, down in its dungeons.'

'Why's there no prison?'

'There's not enough crime. Or hardly any. They don't need a prison. A few holding cells are enough.'

'Why's there no crime?'

'Why do you think? There's no crime because there's only one punishment – hanging. As I said. So everyone's very careful not to commit any.'

'What, just one punishment? Even for . . . well . . . littering?'

'Even for littering. For everything.'

'That's a bit harsh.'

'See any litter though?' Jenine asked.

I looked around. There wasn't a scrap.

'Who else are they hanging tomorrow?' I said.

'Heathens, disbelievers, wrongdoers. Maybe once or twice a year someone does commit a crime. In a fit of anger or a moment of passion or because they've had too much home-made wine. And the authorities save them up to hang them as well.'

'On Quenant's Day?'

'On Quenant's Day. When else? Helps the party go with a swing – as it were.'

I suddenly felt an odd, mad, almost overwhelming urge to take a piece of litter and to throw it on the ground. Just to see what would happen; just to see the looks on people's faces: their outrage, their shock. My hands even went to my pockets, but luckily for me there was no paper in them, or, I do believe, I might really have done it.

Across the square from the cathedral was the town hall. The inevitable gallows and the unavoidable noose were incorporated into a civic coat of arms which glistened on its gabled front like a great medallion.

Two officials came out of the main doors and hurried on their way, their briefcases full of important (or, at least, self-important) business. They were followed by a man and a woman in what must have been police uniforms.

They straightened their tunics, adjusted their hats, then separated and went in different directions. Their uniforms were braided with nooses; their buttonholes were nooses; the epaulettes on their shoulders were nooses too.

'Where now?'

'Just follow.'

We walked around to the rear of the town hall building. Set into the ground at floor level was a metal grille, there to provide light and ventilation, I assumed, for the cellars and dungeons below.

'That's most likely where the prisoners are,' Jenine whispered as we approached. 'We've heard it's where they keep the condemned.'

'The cells? Down there?'

'Yes. That's where you worry and suffer and rot while you're waiting to be strung up.'

We went on walking. I looked down through the grille as we passed by. But all I could make out were some shadowy figures, who could have been prisoners or who could have been jailers, or anyone.

We didn't stop. It might have looked suspicious. We just ambled on, as if we were out-of-towners who had come to the city for Quenant's Day and were taking in the sights.

We circled the building and came back again. Again, we looked down into the cellars. Again there was nothing to see but vague shapes and shadows.

'I think I saw him,' Jenine said. 'I think I saw him.'

But I felt she was seeing what she wanted to, rather than what she actually had.

I couldn't understand how she ever expected to free her father from those cells. I couldn't see how they hoped to save him at all. And I suspected that they had no real idea how to do it either.

But a greater and more immediate problem faced us. For, as we lingered in the main square, watching the scaffold take shape for the following day's 'celebrations' and 'entertainments', it became apparent that there was to be some kind of ghastly dress rehearsal.

A number of armed and uniformed guards appeared and a cry went up of, 'Make way for the prisoners!'

Three men were led out; their faces pale, their arms tied behind them. They were taken to the scaffold, as if to be measured up for tomorrow's executions and to ensure that the whole programme went off smoothly without a hitch. It was a grim and grisly dress rehearsal for death.

The only thing was that Jenine's father was not among them.

'Which one is he?' I asked, as the prisoners were trooped out, for none of the condemned bore any facial scars whatsoever.

'He isn't there.'

'Then where?'

'I don't know. They may . . . have already killed him.'

Her face was ashen; the very scars on it looked pale. She looked at her mother, who looked at Kaneesh, as if to say, Can we already be too late? Can it be true?

'But that's impossible,' I said. 'I thought that executions

were only allowed on Quenant's Day. So how can he have been executed already?'

'They say it's the custom and the law . . .' Jenine said. 'But maybe that's only what they tell people. Who knows what goes on in dungeons and cells?'

I noticed, from the corner of my eye, that one of the beggars on the cathedral steps had gathered up his rags, got creakily to his feet, and was heading in our direction. Kaneesh should never have flipped him that coin, I thought. It had been a mistake for him to draw attention to us, even by a minor act of charity. The beggar was clearly coming towards us. He no doubt wanted more money.

'But if they've already killed him, how do we discover that? We can't just go and not find out,' Jenine said. 'He might still be alive somewhere, for all we know.'

'Perhaps we ought to move on for the moment,' I said nervously. 'We've been standing here too long. People are starting to notice us. Let's walk.'

I glanced back at the approaching beggar. His bowed, hooded head was nodding, as if he had some kind of palsy. People shied away from him, as if the condition were contagious. Which maybe it was. Or perhaps he was simply rotten with vermin.

'Walk on?' Jenine said, indignantly. 'We don't just walk on. We have to find out where my father is. We have to know what happened to him.'

'But it won't help him if we get taken prisoner too,' I pointed out, with what I hoped would seem like calm

242

logic, but which came out sounding more like mounting panic. 'Look, let's just walk on a little. Let's not stand here looking as conspicuous as a bunch of tourists.'

'Let them think we are tourists.'

'Jenine . . . there's someone coming.'

The beggar was but a few steps away. He limped along, supporting himself with a staff, his few tawdry belongings held in a cloth bundle. His hand was already out for money: its permanent position, as likely as not.

'Alms . . . alms . . .'

Kaneesh glared at him.

'Clear off. I gave you alms. Greed kills charity every time. Settle for enough. Forget more.'

'More. More alms.'

All the beggar had to do was to make a fuss. Fuss breeds attention. Attention breeds interest. Interest attracts bystanders. Bystanders attract more bystanders and turn into a small crowd. Which turns into a larger one. Which soon attracts the attention of the authorities. Who would be delighted, no doubt, to have another four non-believers to hang on Quenant's Day.

There might be a reward too, for the finders and the denouncers of non-believers. And a beggar in need of money could always do with a handsome reward.

'Alms, kind sir. More alms. Alms for a poor man.'

'I told you, I just gave you alms. What do you think I am? A pit of money? Be off. Beg somewhere else.' Kaneesh pushed him roughly away. But he just came back.

'Alms, sir. Alms. More alms.'

I reached to take Jenine's arm, to try to steer us away.

'Let's go,' I said. 'Let's just move on.'

She shrugged from my grasp.

'Not until I find where my father is. If he isn't in the cells, where is he?'

The beggar was right by us, close enough to take in every word. I nudged Jenine with my elbow, put my finger to my lips. But it was too late, the beggar had already overheard. And to prove it, he said the most extraordinary and unexpected thing.

'Perhaps, my child,' the beggar said, 'he escaped.'

We stared at him, at his filthy, ragged clothes, at his threadbare, moth-chewed cloak, at his grimy hands, at his face, hidden deep in the shadowed recess of the hood around his head. Two piercing eyes stared out from the darkness.

'Father . . . ?' Jenine said. 'Is that . . . you?'

'Mikhail?' her mother whispered, transfixed by the voice and the appearance of the beggar.

'Brother?' Kaneesh said, his voice trembling. It was the first time since I had met him that I had seen him at a near loss for words or for deeds. Mikhail, is that . . . you? You look filthy.'

'I thought you'd never get here, Kaneesh,' the beggar's voice said. 'What took you so long? And you don't look that clean yourself.'

I thought the game was up then. For I had never seen such visible, true and spontaneous happiness on the faces of people. I thought the whole square was about to erupt in a riot of such an affectionate and tearful reunion that everyone would wonder to see it, that they would stop to watch it, that they would see four scar-faced Cloud Hunters hugging and kissing each other in the way that only those who had believed each other lost or dead can do. I could picture them all but dancing around in celebration. I wouldn't have been surprised if they actually had. Then the next thing would have been the cry of, 'I spy heathens and non-believers!' And then we'd all be up on the scaffold for Quenant's Day.

I had underestimated them.

Barely a flicker. Barely a motion. All that was to come. Time enough to celebrate when there was the safety in which to do it.

'Where is the boat?' Mikhail, the beggar and Jenine's father whispered.

'An hour's walk,' Kaneesh said.

'We'll go ahead and lead the way,' Carla said. 'You follow at a distance, husband. It won't take long.'

But the beggar shook his cowled head.

'Ah no,' he said. 'We cannot leave.'

We stared at him.

'But Father, why ever not?' Jenine said.

He nodded towards the scaffold.

'The other prisoners,' he said. 'We have to take them with us.'

Kaneesh's eyes glittered with anger.

'We came, brother, to save you. Not the whole world. We can't take a hand in everyone's business. We aren't redeemers to save the universe. Just Cloud Hunters, who save their own.'

'No. We save them too. We must. There's no one else to do it.'

'No, brother. We cannot. We cannot take such risks for the sake of strangers. Now we will leave and you must follow – at a discreet distance, so as not to arouse suspicion.'

'I am not leaving my fellow prisoners to their fate,' Mikhail said. 'If it hadn't been for them I would never have escaped myself.'

'It's a hard world, brother. Your thanks will have to suffice. You can burn a candle in their memory, make an offering for their happiness in the afterlife. But we must leave. You must come now.'

'I'll be hanged,' Jenine's father said, 'if I will.'

Kaneesh looked at him.

'You'll be hanged, brother,' he pointed out, 'if you don't.'

Jenine had not told me which of the two brothers was the elder. Was it her father, or was it her uncle? It was hard to tell, for each appeared to be as stubborn and as resolute as the other. Maybe they were twins.

If it had come to a fight between them, I felt they would both have lost and both have won. They'd have died together, still arguing the toss. For they looked like the kind of brothers who would protect each other to the death. If they hadn't fought each other to it first.

34

mikhail's story

'Who's the boy?' Jenine's father wanted to know. 'What's he doing here?'

'Work experience,' Kaneesh said drily – which made me think that he might have a sense of humour after all. Or perhaps his brother just brought out the sarcasm in him.

'He wanted to come along. He's from my school,' Jenine explained.

'And we thought that we might need another pair of hands – to get you out of this place,' Carla said.

We were sitting in a small tea shop.

Jenine's father, the beggar, had abruptly limped away from us as we stood in the square. He must have decided that we were starting to look conspicuous together. So we let him go and then followed at a distance, pretending to be taking in the sights, glancing at the merchandise in shop windows, and feigning interest in the preparations for Quenant's Day. (Although I wasn't feigning; I was interested, and with a horrified fascination.)

Her father led us into a maze of narrow streets. He stopped, glanced back, and disappeared into a small tea shop, which looked neither too expensive, too clean, nor too discerning in its clientele. In fact, if there was a criminal class in this society (and there no doubt was a small one, even with the dire punishment of death for the most trivial of offences looming over their heads and around their necks) then this looked like the sort of establishment where they might (so to speak) hang out.

We went in after the ragged figure and found him already seated at a table.

'Keep your hoods up,' he said, as we joined him. Though this didn't apply to me as my unscarred face didn't need to be covered; I wasn't so obviously from elsewhere. 'They don't mind criminals here, but they're not so keen on foreigners,' he whispered.

(Which showed that even when there is honour among thieves, there is still a certain amount of prejudice against strangers.)

'What'll you have?' he asked, as a waiter approached, his face as dirty as his turban, which was, in its turn, as grimy as his apron, which was also, in its own way, about as filthy as the dish towel he had tucked into it, which was of similar hue to the tablecloth. 'You'd better make it tea,' Mikhail said. 'There's nothing else that's drinkable.'

So tea was what we ordered. And that was when he looked at me and asked again, 'Who's the boy? What's he doing here?'

248

Once we had settled who I was, the others wanted to know how he was and how he had escaped.

'It was simple enough,' he said. 'Easy enough, that is, to get out of the prison. Getting off this blighted island, though, that's another matter. There were four of us condemned men, held in the dungeon cells. Every morning they brought breakfast to us. I arranged with the other prisoners to create a disturbance when my food was brought to me one morning. Which they did. The guard went to settle the trouble between them, leaving my cell door open and unlocked for a moment. I was then supposed to slip out, slit his throat – or strangle him – and free the others.'

He mentioned the throat-slitting and the strangling in a perfectly matter-of-fact, everyday, businesslike tone. And the others nodded in placid agreement. Even Jenine. As if all accepting that such things were a necessary and unavoidable occurrence, and a sadly inevitable component of ordinary life.

'However, just as I was about strangle him – slitting his throat was out of the question, for I had no knife – two of the other guards, who should never have been there, as normally there is only one man to deliver the breakfast, came down the stairs. It was all I could do to fight my way free of them and to get out of the place. I couldn't help my fellow prisoners as intended. But I made it out of the dungeon and onto the street.

'There I was, in the middle of the city, with the guards after me and the alarm sounding and the hue and cry everywhere and shouts of "Escaped prisoner! Escaped prisoner!" echoing in my ears. There wasn't a chance of my making it to the coast or even to the outskirts of the town. Every Believer in the place would be after me. And this place is nothing but Believers – take my word. They don't suffer from doubts in this place. They can't afford to.'

'So what did you do?'

'I did what I had to. There was only one choice. If you cannot run, you must hide. And how, and where, can you hide when your pursuers are but a few corners behind you, about to appear at any second? You hide right under their noses, that's where. Because that's where most people never think to look. For escaped prisoners run, don't they? As fast as their legs will take them. Instinct tells them to do so. And who would not follow his instincts to save his neck?'

'So what happened then, Father?' Jenine said. 'What did you do?'

'I made myself slow down, forced myself to walk. Not to run – to walk. Slowly, deliberately, casually. I pulled up my hood, covered my head, and I walked – with a limp. I saw a stick lying by a wall. I took it and used it as a crutch. Then I hobbled slowly over to the cathedral steps. I could hear the furore behind me. The yelling, the shouting. The guards giving the people in the square rough treatment. "You! A prisoner's escaped. Did you just see a man running? Where did he go?"

'But they hadn't seen a man running. And no one was looking for a poor, lame beggar. So as the commotion continued, I sat myself down on the cathedral steps with all the other mendicants, who squat there all day long, with downcast eyes and miserable expressions – which, need I say, is part of their stock-in-trade. And having downcast eyes, they had seen nothing. They didn't know who I was, or care. I was just another of their kind.

'So there I sat among them, head bowed, eyes lowered, hand out, expression miserable, and I joined in the chorus of, "Alms, Believer. Alms for a poor man." And I've been living that way ever since – while waiting for all of you – ' he spoke sharply and accusingly now, with a measure of long-borne and ill-concealed impatience – 'to turn up. And you took your time.'

'Husband –'

'Brother –'

'Father –'

Mikhail raised his hand for silence. He didn't let them speak another word, and plainly wouldn't until he had finished what he had to say. Maybe he was starved for conversation.

'There is no way off this island by your own efforts, believe me. And I have tried hard enough to get off it. It's impossible. Without a sky-boat of your own you're marooned. All right, you can sky-swim a little way. But how fast and how far can you go without being caught, or before the thermals or the sky-sharks get you?

'So I've been a beggar on the cathedral steps ever since I escaped from the cell. And, irony of ironies, one of those who flings me a coin every once in a while is the very jailer I was going to strangle. So he's not such a bad sort, after all. It's an odd thing, life, don't you think?'

For the first time since I had met him, he smiled.

'Mikhail, we did everything within our power to save you,' Carla said. 'The international courts, the tribunals, we went to them all. We had verdicts in your favour, indictments and decrees. But the Quenant won't pay the slightest attention to any of them. They're a law unto themselves.'

'Fanatics have no interest in any laws other than their own bigotry,' Mikhail said.

'Well, we're here now,' Jenine said.

'And the boat is under an hour away. We could be on it and out of this place before the midday bell,' Kaneesh reminded him.

'I made an agreement,' Jenine's father said, with calm, resolute insistence. 'We shook hands on it. Those other three prisoners – they would help me to escape, and I would help them. I gave them,' he said, 'my word – as a Cloud Hunter.'

Kaneesh's jaw twitched, then his expression became set, as if in stone. That statement had clinched it. The matter was beyond dispute. His brother had given his word as a Cloud Hunter. What could be more binding than that?

Yet, admire as I did Mikhail's honour and integrity, I couldn't help but think to myself that I hadn't given my word, not as a Cloud Hunter or as anything. And neither had anybody else, just Jenine's father.

It didn't seem fair to me that we would probably all be

252

caught and hanged now, just because he had made a promise. I didn't see how we could possibly free those prisoners without getting taken ourselves.

The city was a mass of Believers by then, with more arriving every hour. Already people were marking their spots out in the square so that they might have a fine view of tomorrow's executions. They had come prepared to camp out overnight to secure their places.

Yes, outside, I thought, was a potential lynch mob, a hundred thousand strong. So I didn't rate our chances of rescue and escape very highly. I didn't rate them at all.

'Anyone want more of this tea?' Mikhail asked.

I nodded.

'Thanks,' I said. 'Wouldn't mind another cup.'

Anything to delay the moment. From a limited number of options, more tea seemed like the best available.

Yet, for some reason, Jenine was smiling.

35

rescue plan

Three of us left the tea shop: Kaneesh, myself and Jenine.
Her parents said they would follow after five minutes,
and so we threaded our way back along the streets and
alleyways and out into the countryside, to return to the
secluded cove and the hidden ship, bobbing at anchor in
the air.

By now the entire populace of the island seemed to be
heading into the city for the following day's 'festivities'
– if that was the correct word for a public hanging. Anxious
to remain inconspicuous, we unavoidably stood out from
the crowd by the very fact of our going against it. We
were swimmers against the tide.

'Where are you going, Believer? You're heading the
wrong way! You surely don't want to miss the fun!'

(Fun, indeed? I thought. People being hanged is fun?
Which only went to show that one person's misery is only
too often another's entertainment.)

People jostled and cajoled us, already in a light-hearted,

party mood. Kaneesh bristled, as if he'd like to knock some heads together, but discretion held him back.

The alleyways widened into streets and the streets turned to country roads. We reached the track we had come along and retraced our steps. We found the boat, still safe and hidden, and climbed aboard to wait for the others.

They took their time and were late enough to worry us, but eventually they came, arm-in-arm. No doubt they had had plenty to talk about and much to say to each other along the way.

Kaneesh was preparing a meal when they arrived. But the instant we sat down to eat it, he raised the subject that was at the back of all of our minds.

'So, brother,' he said, 'these friends of yours –'

'Fellow prisoners,' Mikhail corrected him. ('Friends' evidently might have been exaggerating the case a little and pitching it too strong.)

'Well, however you describe them, you seem to have some strange loyalty to them. And if you've given your word that they will be rescued, then so be it. But let me point something out to you. Right now they are held in a dungeon in a crowded city, which grows busier by the minute. Tomorrow, these three men are to be hanged in front of thousands – tens of thousands. There are five of us. Two men. One woman. One girl. And a useless boy who is not even a Cloud Hunter.'

(I slightly resented the 'useless boy' part of that. But I had never before heard Kaneesh string so many sentences together and was interested to hear what would come next.

He was normally a man of few words, but had now grown suddenly eloquent.)

'So how exactly are we to rescue these three friends of yours, brother?' he went on. 'Five of us against a hundred thousand or more? Not good odds. Even for Cloud Hunters.'

Mikhail was pensive and took his time to reply.

'It needs some thought,' he conceded.

'I doubt we have enough time for all the thought it will need,' Kaneesh observed. 'They're hanging them tomorrow. By the time we work out a way of saving them, they'll need cremating.'

His brother glared at him, but said nothing.

Then Carla spoke. 'I may have a solution,' she said.

Her husband and brother-in-law looked at her dubiously. It crossed my mind that maybe things were a little difficult for her now. Since Mikhail had been taken prisoner, she had captained the ship – with Kaneesh to assist her, true – but she had been in charge. Now Mikhail was back he would no doubt wish to resume his authority; but maybe she would not wish to relinquish hers. Perhaps from now on there would not be one captain for the boat, but a joint – or endlessly disputed – command.

'And what solution is that?' Mikhail asked.

'This boat of ours,' Carla said, 'is a sky-boat – correct?'

'Of course.'

'With a rounded hull for buoyancy, which prevents it from ever landing and keeps it air-bound. It has to dock and tie up. It cannot land on solid earth the way a sky-barge might.'

256

'And?'

'But the fact it cannot come down to land does not prevent it sailing over land, or under it, or around it . . .'

'And?' Kaneesh said, increasingly impatient.

'So it is quite possible for us to sail from here to Quenant City. To sail over and above the cathedral in the city square – over tomorrow's crowds, in fact.'

'And?'

'And who will be expecting that?' she said. 'Who will be expecting a ship to appear right over their heads – right over the gibbet, right over the scaffold, right at the moment when . . .'

Mikhail and Kaneesh looked at each other, and then at Carla, with a grudging, and possibly reluctant, admiration.

'It's a thought,' Kaneesh nodded.

'It is a thought,' Mikhail agreed.

'It's more than a thought. It's the best idea we have,' Jenine pointed out. 'In fact, it's the only idea.' And I felt she was right. But made no comment. It's best to stay out of other people's family affairs. (Sometimes it's best to stay out of family affairs even when it's your own family. Especially when, on some occasions.)

'Does anyone have any other suggestions?' Carla asked.

But – judging from the silence – they did not.

We slept badly that night. I certainly did. When I opened my eyes to see other eyes as wide open as my own, I didn't feel so bad about my nervousness. Thoughts of tomorrow prevented us all from sleeping, except in fits and starts. It always seems to be the way that when you most need rest because of what is ahead of you, then what is ahead of you stops you getting any.

We ate an early breakfast then we cast off. Clouds were mustering not far offshore, so we headed for them to replenish the water tanks. Then we made course again, back to the Forbidden Isles and on to the city of Quenant.

Kaneesh was at the wheel. He tilted the rudder and the boat angled upwards. As we sailed over the coastal areas we ascended. Higher and higher we rose, still moving inland. The city of Quenant grew visible in the distance, but we went on ascending until the metropolis was little more than a toy town directly beneath us. Had I dropped a stone over the side of the boat, it would have landed smack bang in the middle of the cathedral square.

Jenine took the binoculars and peered over the side.

'Look,' she said. 'You can see the gallows. They're up and finished. Everything's ready.'

We could see both the gallows and the gathering crowds below us. The square was filled with the faithful, crammed shoulder to shoulder, waiting patiently for the execution hour of noon.

We waited. Mikhail checked the water hoses. Kaneesh was tending to the mooring ropes, knotting their dangling ends into sliding nooses, the kind you could use to loop around a capstan – or even around a man.

Still we waited. There was nothing else to do or to be done; no other means of occupying the time other than patiently waiting and watching through the binoculars and telescope.

Finally, it was ten minutes to noon. Then the chime of midday rang out.

'Here they come,' Kaneesh said. He handed the telescope to his brother. He looked down, then nodded.

'Let's descend.'

Carla, at the helm, angled the boat down.

We sailed down, smoothly and silently. The breeze was cool upon our faces. The insects in the square turned into people; the toy, miniature buildings became life-size and real. The little needlepoints of the cathedral became magnificent spires.

The city square was packed. People stood on carts, looked out from windows, crowded onto balconies, all desiring a glimpse of the gallows on the podium and of the prisoners about to be hanged in honour of Quenant the Martyr and all that he stood for – whatever it was.

Here the prisoners came: three men, their arms tied behind them; walking solemnly, and not without courage, to their deaths. Not without courage, but not without fear either. For without fear, there is no courage. How can there be, when courage is fear overcome?

We descended swiftly now, sailing down and in from behind the crowd. Nobody had seen us – yet.

A robed priest stood upon the gallows' podium, intoning what he, no doubt, regarded as a few apt and significant words.

'Oh blessed Quenant,' he proclaimed, 'we offer these wrongdoers to your mercy. Forgive their transgressions. Allow them to have the honour of your martyr's death. As you died for the faith, let them die for their sins, so that they may be absolved. May the rope be strong and the gallows be sound. May the death be quick or the death be long, as is your will. In the name of . . .'

He made the sign of the noose. The crowd in the square did the same in response. The guards and the hooded hangman ushered the prisoners forwards. Three dangling nooses waited for the three condemned men. It was just a matter of putting those nooses around their necks, the blindfolds around their eyes, the weights around their ankles, then pulling the trapdoor levers. But . . .

'Look! Look! Look!'

We were seen by one pair of eyes. In an instant we were seen by all.

'Dive!' Kaneesh shouted. 'Dive!'

Down we went. All we had was surprise, our sole, valuable element. If we lost that now, we lost everything.

Our ropes were at the ready, dangling over the side. Two rope ladders were also flung over, from fore and aft.

We were there at the scaffold, hovering right above it. Mikhail was clambering down one of the rope ladders, a dagger in his hand. Kaneesh was at the other ladder, a dagger in his hand also, and his new, second knife between his teeth. Carla kept the helm steady. Jenine and I held the water cannon. Jenine turned it on. A cascade of water shot out at maximum pressure and highest speed.

We aimed the jet down and hosed the running guards clean off their feet. They slipped and slithered and scrambled around the podium. Kaneesh and Mikhail were by now running and scrambling along the podium too. They lost their balance, regained it. The guards drew swords and daggers. The crowd advanced, shouting angrily, funnelling up the steps, sensing that the day's long-awaited entertainment was about to be snatched from before their eyes.

'Archers!' a voice cried. 'Arrows! Arrows and guns!'

The prisoners ran, slipping and sliding. They ran to their salvation, towards the dangling rope ladders and our hovering ship. But they couldn't climb the ladders for their hands were tied behind them. Kaneesh freed one set of hands, Mikhail another. Those prisoners scurried up the ropes, Kaneesh and Mikhail behind them. The guards and the screaming crowd were almost upon them. There was no time to cut the third prisoner free.

'Ascend! Up! Up!'

Carla began to take the boat up. The guards were climbing the rope ladders towards us. Kaneesh cut the tethers. The ladders fell to the podium, and the guards with them.

'The other prisoner!' Jenine shouted. 'Use one of the mooring ropes!'

I left her to handle the water cannon. She blasted a guard with it, who was still hanging onto the boat. He fell to earth with a bone-shattering crunch.

I dangled a mooring rope over the side. I prayed to all

the gods that I did, and did not, believe in that my aim would be good and true.

It was. I got him. Hooked him tight. My noose fell over the third prisoner's head and chest. Then, as we ascended, the rope slid on its slip knot, tightened under his arms, and pulled him up with us. He cried out in pain, the noose around his chest crushing the breath out of him. But we soon got him on board.

'Full power! Go!' Mikhail shouted.

Beneath us was an ocean of angry faces. Arrows rose into the sky. Some thwacked into the boat. There was the crack of gunshot. You could hear the bullets as they ricocheted off the bulwarks, or embedded themselves into the hull. But soon, even they could no longer reach us. Some of the angry crowd tried to air-swim after us, but they didn't get far. It's one thing to swim off the coast or from a boat, but to swim up far from solid land is beyond even the strongest.

'Aren't they coming after us?' I asked Jenine. For no ships seemed to be following.

'Of course they are,' she said. 'Look! There they come!'

Far down beneath us, boats were rising into the sky, angling up in pursuit.

'Empty the water tanks,' Mikhail yelled. 'We'll outrun them!'

The last of the water trickled from the cannon. The wind sails opened fully, the spinnaker yawned wide; the solar engines took up every last watt of energy that they could extract from the sun.

We rode the thermals like a skimming stone. We bounced

and flitted, we sped and flew, fast as sky-fish fleeing from a sky-shark, and on we sailed across the Great Divide. Soon we had lost them. The pursuing ships were motes of dust in a beam of sunlight; the Isle of Quenant was a distant rock.

They wouldn't catch us now. We were at liberty, where – with luck – we would remain. The three rescued prisoners sat there on the deck and smiled. I saw that one of them was massaging his neck, as if surprised to find it still there in one piece.

I joined Jenine at the stern of the boat.

'What about the man who took your father prisoner?' I said. 'I thought you all wanted to be revenged on him. I thought you wanted to cut his throat. Or hang him, the way he'd tried to hang that dog.'

She gave me a smile.

'As long as my father's back – what does it matter? And anyway, hanging's too good for some people, don't you think?'

She turned and stared back at the islands.

'You usually sit at the prow,' I said. 'At the front of the boat, not the back.'

'Yes,' she said. 'I usually like to see where we're going. But sometimes . . .'

'Sometimes what?'

'Sometimes,' she said, 'it's nice to see where you've been. To remember what you did. Sometimes it's nice to look back.'

I couldn't disagree with that. So I sat beside her, and looked back too.

36

home

'What did they do?' I asked. 'To warrant hanging?'

The boat seemed somewhat crowded now. There had been four of us when we set off, now there were eight – twice as many and half as much deck space. There was twice as much stew to cook and twice as many bowls to wash. Somehow the washing-up had again fallen to me.

'The other three prisoners, you mean?' Jenine said.

'Yes. The ones the Quenant were going to hang along with your father. What had they done to deserve it?'

'Well, one let his dog mess on the footpath, and forgot to clean it up,' Jenine said. I thought at first that she was joking, but she wasn't.

'And they were going to hang him for that?' I said.

'They were going to hang the dog too. It turns out that it was the dog my father tried to rescue.'

'And the other two?'

'One left his handcart in a no parking area.'

'And the third?'

'He tried to kill the President, on the grounds that he was an unelected tyrant.'

'What's going to happen to them now?'

'Well, they're on the run, aren't they? So that more or less makes them Dissenters.'

'Depending on how you look at it.'

'It's how we're looking at it. And they seem to agree. So we're going to drop them off at the Isles of Dissent. They can go on from there. If they don't like Hippy Isle, they can cadge a ride to one of the other islands. There's usually one to suit everybody.' She looked at me. 'There might even be one where you'd fit in.' She grinned.

'Thanks.'

'You're welcome.'

'I might of course –' I said tentatively, after a pause '– fit in here.'

She thought it over, then shook her head.

'I don't think so, Christien,' she said. 'To fit in here you first have to fit in nowhere else. And you already have a home. And you'd also need a couple of scars on your face. I think you're better off without those.'

She got up and went down to the cabins, leaving me with the washing-up.

We docked at Hippy Isle in the Isles of Dissent. I wouldn't say that the people there exactly gave a warm and enthusiastic welcome to the new arrivals we deposited on the quay; the locals were too laid-back to be enthusiastic about anything. But they were friendly enough towards them.

'Ah, right, man,' said the harbour master, a tall, long-haired individual, whose head was in a permanent swathe of mist from the pipe he was smoking. 'Yeah, right. Quenant, right?' he went on. 'Going to hang you, man? Yeah. Crazy. Well, well. Evil scene, man. Bad vibe. Well out of it, man. Yeah, you can crash here, no worries. Just go downtown, man, and say the harbour master sent you. You should find a squat there, in one of the communes or somewhere, man. No worries, my friend. Yeah. Right. Just take it easy, dudes. Peace, man. Cool.'

Then he looked at Jenine's family, at their scarred faces and at their tattoos, at their plaited hair, at the medallions around their necks, at the gold bands upon their arms and wrists and ankles, and he exhaled a plume of smoke and said admiringly, 'Cloud Hunters, eh, man? Cool, man. Cool.' He caught sight of me and said, 'You a Cloud Hunter too, man?'

I waited for somebody else to deny it. But they left me to answer for myself. So I nodded my head a little and said, 'Sort of.'

And he said, 'Cool, man. Cool thing to be.'

And so it was. I didn't disagree.

We said goodbye to the rescued prisoners. They shouted their thanks and waved their farewells as our boat sailed away into the main thermals and as we turned for home – well, my home. The Cloud Hunters already were at home; their boat was their home. So they were always at home, and never at home too; for they had neither land

266

nor country; they were eternal wanderers of the sky, who were born and who lived and who died there. They were creatures of another element. Not like the rest of us, with our boring, steady feet on the solid, unshakeable ground. They were creatures of the air, like sky-fish, except they had no wings. Their boats were their wings, and the sails were their feathers and scales. They were born to soar, to be free.

We returned by the Main Drift, only diverting from it once to pursue a cloud bank which appeared off to starboard. We headed for it, turned the compressors on and filled the tanks. Then, with a full hold, we set course to my home island.

'How many days?' I asked Kaneesh.

'Two,' he said. 'Three, maybe.'

Two days. Three at most. And it would all be over.

My eyes searched the sky for sight of a sky-whale, or maybe a stinger, or a ship full of dangerous Barbaroons. But no. We sailed on safely and quietly. It seemed that we had run out of adventures.

As we were nearing the last day, Jenine came to me and said, 'Do you want to swim again?'

I suppose it was a way of saying goodbye – a last pleasure, a last treat before the holiday was over.

'Yes,' I said. 'That would be good.'

They stopped the boat. We dived over and swam and floated in the air. I was getting good at this, I felt, and wasn't afraid any more of falling any more, or of the great depths beneath me.

As we swam, two sky-fins came along, and they seemed to want to play. They nudged us with their rubbery snouts and we grabbed onto the humped fins on their backs as they sped and cavorted through the sky, turning somersaults and cartwheels as we held on tight, laughing and shouting and happy, as if life were a joy that could never end.

After a while the sky-fins stopped and seemed to want some reward. Carla threw them a handful of dried sky-fish from the boat; they gobbled it all up and swam contentedly on.

Then we had to move on too.

'Are you coming back to school, for the next term?' I asked Jenine as my home island came into sight in the distance.

'I don't know,' she said. 'It depends on my father. I think he wants to move on. He says this part of the sky is played out and overworked. He's heard it's better elsewhere.'

But I thought to myself that nomads must always believe that – that things are better elsewhere. It gives them reason to be moving on; it justifies and legitimises their restless natures.

'But you'll stay for a while?' I said.

'Maybe.'

37

unexpected honours

When we came back on board, there was a reception committee waiting: Kaneesh and Jenine's mother and father were all standing there, looking solemn and ominous, and I wondered what was up.

It was Mikhail who kicked things off.

'Christien,' he said. 'My young friend. We have been talking between us and have agreed that we have much to thank you for. Without your help, who knows, I and three others might be now dangling from a string on the Isle of Quenant.'

'I think you'd have managed without me,' I said. (And not from any false modesty. I believed they would have.)

'All the same,' Mikhail continued. 'You have our thanks. We are not material people, as you'll have seen. We don't have much by way of possessions or by way of wealth. The honours we confer are not expensive gifts. But we have our own ways of showing our gratitude.'

I did wonder what they might be. But then something

told me. I smelt the herbs, bubbling in the small pot on top of the brazier. I saw the ceremonial knife, warming up in the heat, its tip just starting to glow red. I saw the phial in Carla's hand, like the one the mother of Alain, the young Cloud Hunter, had broken open, and the numbing contents of which she had poured into his drink, just before they had –

And my heart sank. It sank all the way down to the sun.

Jenine realised too. She stared at me. Not just into my eyes, but right down into my heart, to my very secret self. And she knew, just as I did, with, I'm sure, the same regret and sadness, what my answer would be to the question about to be asked.

'We would,' Mikhail continued, 'like to accord you the greatest honour we can offer to you, my young friend, by way of our thanks. With your permission, if you are happy to accept them, we would like you to receive – the scars.'

What could I say? What could I do? It wasn't the fear; it wasn't the thought of the pain; it wasn't the permanent disfigurement; it wasn't any of those things. Hadn't I thought to myself how much I wanted those scars, on so many occasions? How I would look with them, what a cool, impressive person I would be.

Jenine kept staring at me. She knew, as well as I did, that if I chose to have those scars, then I chose her too. I would be like them, with them, of them, forever. We could grow together, be together. All that she had held back, she

270

would no longer keep from me. We would belong to each other. All I had to do was say the right words.

And I couldn't. I couldn't say them. I wanted to. I did. So much. So much. But I too had a family, a home, a mother, a father, uncles, aunts. I couldn't. If I returned home with those scars etched forever into my face –

I couldn't do it to them. I just couldn't. Much as I – so much as I –

I just couldn't.

I don't really remember what I said. I know that it must have been the right kind of thing because no one was offended. I thanked them all for the huge honour that had been offered to me. I thanked them for their hospitality, for having allowed me to join them. I said, yes, all the right things. And I declined to have those scars put onto my face. I hoped they would understand my reasons, and they seemed to. And we drank some green tea. I was actually getting to like it.

But Jenine went and stood alone by the deck rail. And she wouldn't look at me. But then, when we set sail again, I went over to her and said,

'Jenine – you do understand –?'

She looked at me now.

'I understand, Christien. You can't be what you're not. And neither can I. And for that reason –'

'That doesn't mean we can't be – be friends.'

'No,' she said. 'It doesn't mean we can't be friends. But we can never be more than that now, can we? My

271

face is scarred. And yours is not. And that puts a world between us.'

'It doesn't. It needn't. That's not true. We can still –'

'It does, Christien. You chose home. Your people. Your life. Just as I would choose mine. In fact, neither of us even has a choice. You can't be a Cloud Hunter. And I can't not be. And that's how it is.'

And I think that she was crying. But I couldn't really tell you. I couldn't really see so well. For my own eyes were a little blurred. I don't recollect why.

'You'll all have to come and visit us,' I said, as my home island came into sight. 'Have a meal with us. All of you. With me and my parents. They'll want to thank you all – for taking me and for bringing me back. And we can tell them everything that happened – well, maybe not all of it, we can miss out the more dangerous bits. But some of it. I mean, things like that don't happen every day, do they?'

'Don't they?' Jenine said to me.

But maybe for her they did.

The nearer we got to my island, the less I wanted to go home. I wanted to see my parents again, of course. But it's still sad when things end – things that you don't want to end. And I wanted this to go on forever: sailing the skies, finding clouds and selling water to all the distant, strange, parched and thirsty islands that make up this wonderful world in which we live.

People who have not been here would no doubt say that a world like ours was a scientific impossibility, that

272

it defied all the known laws of gravity and atmosphere, and could not possibly exist.

But do you know something? It was the same in the old world too. It's the same with every world. They're all miracles. Given the facts and the chances at the outset, most people would say it's not possible; such worlds, such people could never come about. Yet here the world is. Here we are, living in it. The chances against us being here are billions to one. But we breathe, we exist. We might not even understand it ourselves yet. We might never understand it. But here we are.

The closer we got to my home, the less Jenine and I seemed to have to say to each other. It was as if the Cloud Hunters were travelling away from me and in their minds were already taking their leave. I was no longer a friend and a companion. I had become a landlubbing stranger again, one of 'them', one of the land-dwellers, with no understanding of their customs or their nomadic lives.

And then we were tying up at the harbour. The few things I had brought with me were packed in my bag.

'I'll be back in the morning,' I said to them. 'To let you know what time to come to dinner tomorrow. Is that all right?'

The others looked to Mikhail. He neither nodded nor shook his head, but just said, 'Of course. And thank you again, my friend, for all you have done.'

Jenine's mother said goodbye, and I thanked her for having me on board. Her father shook my hand and grasped my shoulder and said that he was pleased to have met me and he thanked me for my help – though I protested that I had done little enough and had been more of a passenger and a burden than anything else.

And then Kaneesh said goodbye.

'So you're leaving us, boy,' he said.

'Yes, but you'll all be coming to visit tomorrow,' I said. 'My parents will want to meet you all and to thank you.'

'Here,' he said. 'Take this.'

I looked at his hand. One of his daggers was held in it. Its blade gleamed in the light and the jewelled hilt sparkled.

'But I . . . it's your knife.'

'It's yours now,' he said. 'So use it wisely. Don't cut too many compression tubes with it, eh? Or too many throats.'

'I won't.'

'You didn't do badly, boy,' Kaneesh said. 'You didn't do badly at all.'

From him, high praise indeed.

He put the hilt of the knife into my hand and clasped my own hand around it, then he turned his back and walked away.

There was only Jenine to say goodbye to now.

'Here,' she said. 'That's for you too.'

She took one of the thin gold bands from around her wrist and she put it around mine.

And I knew right then that I would never now see her again. I knew that when I came back in the morning, they would be gone.

'Jenine . . .' I said. 'I don't have anything to give you –'

But she just put a finger up to my lips.

274

'Yes, you do,' she said.

And, of course, she was right. So I leaned forward, and I kissed her, and I held her in my arms, held her tightly, and she held me too, and I said all the words I'd wanted to say to her for so long, from since I'd first set eyes on her.

We must have stood there like that a long time, because I remember hearing someone clearing their throat and I glanced up and saw Kaneesh and Carla and Mikhail, all studiously looking at anything but the two of us, locked in each other's arms.

And then I had to go.

I climbed up the walkway and onto the dockside. Carla passed me my bag. I said goodbye and I thanked them yet again, and then I started to walk. My house wasn't far, no more than fifteen minutes' walk away.

I looked back many times and I waved to them again and again. Then I turned along the cliff path that led to my house and I could no longer see them. All I could see was the mast of the boat and the solar sails.

In another few minutes, I was home.

They were happy to see me. And I was glad to see them too.

'But look at you,' my mother said. 'Look how tanned you are. How dark you've got. And your hair's grown. And with that dagger in your belt and that bracelet around your arm, you know what you look like . . .'

I knew just what I looked like.

275

'He looks like some kind of disreputable Cloud Hunter,' my father said with a chuckle.

And it was just the right thing to say to me. He couldn't have given me a better welcome home.

I went to see them, early the following morning, to give them their invitation to come and eat with us. But it was too late, they were already gone, as I knew they would be.

They must have set off first thing, to catch the solar tide. I walked home, my heart heavy, my footsteps dragging. Jenine and her family had gone.

But I guess I had known that from the very beginning. I had known it all along. Cloud Hunters never stay anywhere for long; they must always be moving. It's in their nature, in their blood. They are like the very clouds they follow, perpetually drifting and moving with the wind and tide. And if you want to go with them, you have to become one of them – completely, without compromise.

I think they chase the clouds the way we chase our dreams. The next one is always the best – the one not yet fully formed, the next cloud, the next dream. That is what we all pursue, one way or another.

When I got home my mother was getting ready to leave for work. She could see from my face that I had missed them, the disappointment was plain to read. She tried to be consoling and sympathetic, but she was a little bit victorious too, vindicated, as if all her warnings had been proved correct – that everything she had always said about

Cloud Hunters had been right. They were fickle, strange, undependable, unpredictable, and always moving on.

'See,' she couldn't help herself saying, 'I told you it wouldn't last. And now they've gone. Without so much as a goodbye. I mean, what in the end did you get out of it all? Buffeted and knocked halfway around the Main Drift, your father and me driven mad with worry, and all for what?'

All for what?

Well, I could have said many things. I could have told her that there was nothing I would have exchanged those weeks for. It made a memory for me, one to last forever. Yes, I could have said so many things, but she would never really have understood.

'What did you get out of it all, you see?' she said. 'All that danger and discomfort and all the rest. What did you get out of it? What did you actually get?'

She left to go to work.

'What did you get?'

What did I get?

What did I get? I got a dagger and a bracelet and unforgettable memories.

I raised my fingers and I touched my lips.

'And a kiss,' I whispered. 'I got a kiss.'

But I don't think my mother heard me say that; she had already closed the door.

You know, I think that there are scars on my face, of a kind. It wasn't a knife that put them there. It was experience and time. You need special eyes to see them. But they're there.

38

tomorrow

Somewhere, in this vast and wonderful world of islands and sky, a small boat plies its trade, searching for clouds, hunting them down, condensing them, selling the water. There is a girl on board with jet-black hair and the most beautiful brown skin, and with two deep facial scars running from under her eyes down towards her mouth. You might think that such scars would make her look less pretty than she is, but they don't. If anything they made her look even more beautiful and mysterious and . . .

Oh well.

On the boat sails, on into the sky. There's a far cloud forming, you can see it, some fifty kilometres away, cotton wool in a pale blue sky. The boat turns and heads for it. They'll be with it in a couple of hours. If somebody else doesn't get there first.

Yes, on that boat is a girl with deep green eyes. I'll probably never see her again. But I kissed her once, and she kissed me back. And I held her in my arms. You never forget a thing like that. Never. I think I was a little in love with her, but I couldn't say for sure. No. That's not true. I was in love with her. I still am. I always will be. I think she maybe loved me too.

Her mother is singing as they sail; it's a sad sort of song, but tender too, almost a kind of lament, a lullaby. It would send the shivers up your spine and bring tears to your dry, indifferent eyes.

The boat glides on, on the solar wind, until at last it comes to the bank of cloud. It floats on into it, is enveloped by it, and gradually fades from view.

Finally, it disappears.

And you wouldn't even know it was there at all.

You wouldn't know that it had ever existed.

The Cloud Hunters have been swallowed by the clouds.

One day, when I'm older, I'll sail the world. I'll go to all the places there are to go to and see everything there is to see. I'll sail the known islands and I'll go on travelling to find new ones. And new ones after that. And the worlds beyond, that no one has even discovered, and I'll see things that no one has yet seen.

And there will never be an end to it all, never an end to the journey.

Never an end to the wide, wide world.

Not even an end on the day I die.

Only ever a new beginning.

And who knows, but that before that, I may even find her again. If someone else hasn't found her first.

Maybe even now, she's thinking about me, as the clouds gather around her, like halos in the sky. Remembering me, the way I remember her. And always will do. Yes. Always will.

Alex Shearer

Alex Shearer was born in Wick, in the far north of Scotland. His father was a blacksmith and his mother was a secretary. He enjoyed writing from an early age, and sold his first television script about thirty years ago. He went on to write several TV series, stage plays, radio plays and comedy scripts. Moving into writing for children, his novels BOOTLEG and THE GREATEST STORE IN THE WORLD were adapted for television by the BBC, and his 2003 novel THE SPEED OF THE DARK was shortlisted for the Guardian Children's Fiction Prize. He lives in Somerset and is married with two grown-up children.